MONEY WOMAN

BASED ON TRUE EVENTS

SINMISOLA OGÚNYINKA,
RICHARDS C. AKONAM

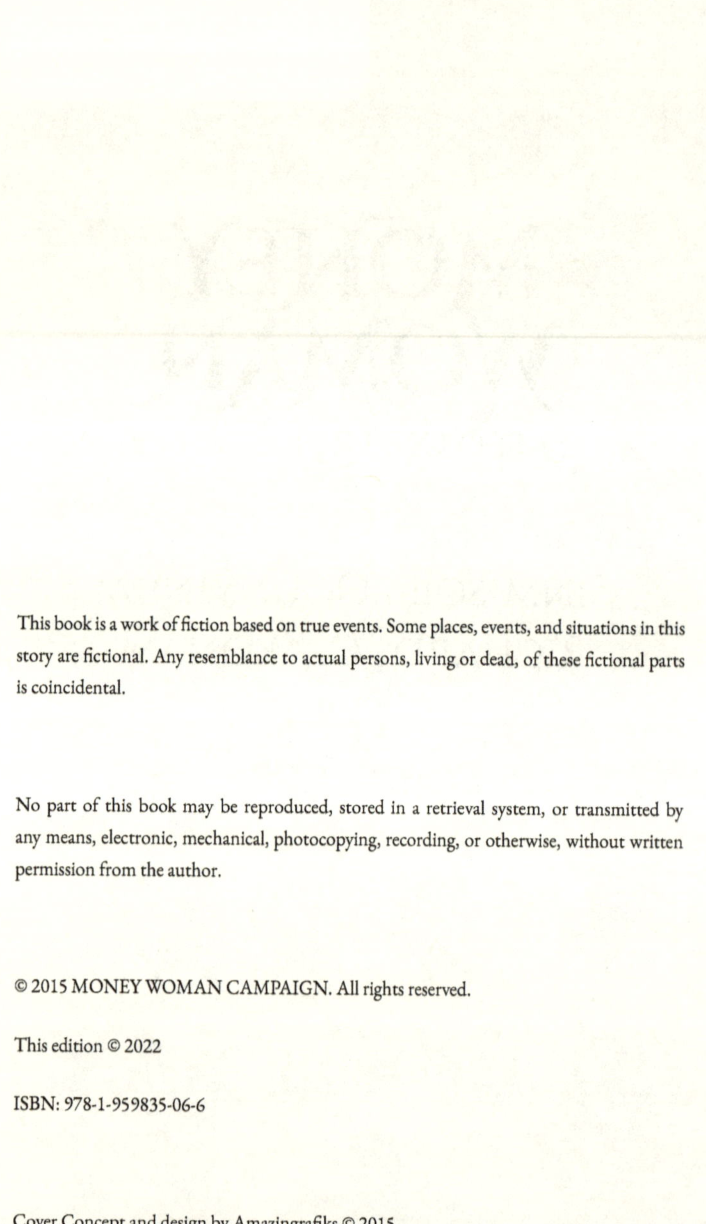

This book is a work of fiction based on true events. Some places, events, and situations in this story are fictional. Any resemblance to actual persons, living or dead, of these fictional parts is coincidental.

No part of this book may be reproduced, stored in a retrieval system, or transmitted by any means, electronic, mechanical, photocopying, recording, or otherwise, without written permission from the author.

Cover Concept and design by Amazingrafiks © 2015

Dedicated to the campaign.

PART I

ROSE

CHAPTER ONE

R ose walks the elderly sick woman to her private room in the newly renovated Hope Hospital, Calabar. She drops her lab coat on the lone visitor's chair and sets the woman down on it before she straightens the bed.

"Okay, come here." Rose gestures and the woman stands feebly. Rose reaches out quickly. "Easy, easy. Sorry."

"Thank you, my child," the woman says with a feathery voice.

Rose lowers her on to the bed and she moans. Then she arranges her legs and dress, and folds the wrapper the woman carried with her, by one side of the bed.

"Don't pick any calls. You need to rest."

The woman moans. "I've heard. Thank you."

Rose walks to the window and draws the blinds. She peers at the patient. The woman's eyes are closed. She adjusts the covering cloth on the woman, picks her lab coat and walks out of the room.

—

Ashi walks toward the new wing of private wards, toward the doctors' room. It's been a long day for him, and he badly needs a cup of coffee. The works done on the hospital recently has made more amenities available for better medical services at the Hope Hospital, one of which is the coffee percolator in the doctors' room.

The corridor is wide enough to take a chariot now, and he's pleased with his new work environment. He approaches a room with the door wide open and slows. Someone might be coming out of the room and he isn't ready to collide. Involuntarily he peeps into the room and stops at the sight before him. What first catches his attention is the waistline of the caregiver. And her backside. Ashi isn't into women but this lady has a nice shape. He will his legs to continue but instead stares as the lady walks over to the curtain and draws it close.

Ashi steals a glance at the sick woman. Her eyes are close. Could the young one be her daughter? With the recent expansion in the hospital, there have been a lot of new faces both staff and patient. In the recent past, he probably would have known who this patient was.

The lady turns and not ready to be caught gawking, Ashi steps back on to the corridor. Miss Pretty Shape steps out a nanosecond afterward, and Ashi gasps. Her face is free of any make up except probably a lip gloss, but her smooth fair skin glows. She turns for a second and peers at the patient and then gently closes the door.

Ashi is grateful she faces away from him. Or she'll have bumped into him. She gets a firmer grip on her lab coat and faces the direction Ashi was headed. Ashi hesitates and uses the moment to admire her. She's clothed in a simple fitted grey suit that outlines her curves in a classy way. Her hair is woven stylishly with extensions that blend with her dark brown hair colour. Besides that, and flat office shoes, Miss Pretty just is pretty.

"Are you new?"

The words are out of Ashi's mouth before he knows. The receding figure in front of him stops. She turns around slowly.

"Um, yes sir. Um—"

Ashi leans against the wall and folds his arms. "A nurse?" He glances at her lab coat. It doesn't seem likely but then he doesn't think a doctor would straighten the bed for a patient.

"I'm actually doing my clinicals, sir."

Ashi frowns. "Clinicals?"

"Yes. I'm from UCTH actually, but since school is on break, my friends and I decided to work here as volunteers," she says.

This grabs Ashi's interest. A hard-working beautiful student. "Ohho. Student nurse?"

"No, sir. Emm, medical—medicine."

Ashi walks toward her and stops short of violating her personal space. "I see. I'm Dr. Ashi Anusa." He holds out his hand to her.

She looks at his hand and gasps. "Dr. Anusa? You own this hospital?"

Her question amuses Ashi but he doesn't want to laugh at her. She has a right to assume. His lips tilts up in a half-smile. "My Dad." He shrugs. "But we work here together."

She looks nervously at his outstretched hand, and curtseys instead. "Hello, you're welcome sir."

Ashi chuckles, unable to hold it, and slowly pockets his hand. "I see you're very committed to your work. Well done."

She curtseys again. "Thank you, sir."

"What's your name?"

"Rose."

"Beautiful name. Will you be like that beautiful flower to me?" Ashi wants to rub his hands together but that would

seem too suggestive. He didn't hit on women so easily.

"I'm not sure I have that capacity, sir," Rose says, her lips tremble slightly.

Ashi likes her shyness but he wants her to snap out of it. "Call me Ashi."

CHAPTER TWO

18 YEARS AGO

In the early hours of the morning, when the cock is yet to crow, in a slum area with face-me-I-face-you rooms, the front door crashes open and Ezor, a stocky man in his late thirties stumble out on to the dirt floor, clutching a wrapper tied to his waist. His fat wife who is almost half his age stumbles out of the room in a dramatic fashion.

Ezor turns and lunges at her. She grabs his head, thrust into her midriff and nearly knocking breath out of her, and struggles to push him back on the ground. The effort forces them both to the ground, with Ezor under obese weight. Ezor punches her flabby waist as her continued pressure makes him dizzy. If she doesn't release him soon, he will faint. Neighbours shout curses from every direction but none bother to leave their rooms to intervene.

Ezor finally succumbs and goes limp beneath her. She

stands a little and then drops on him for a finishing effect, and cursing in her local Efik dialect, goes back into the room and locks the door.

—

Ezor gets down from a bus on a dirt road and walks down a track into Kundeve village. A few children run to him and carry his bag and dance around him. He enters a cement-plastered and green-painted house. His mother and father soon come out rejoicing over him.

After a couple of hours of rest, he goes in search of Mam, his widowed cousin who lives in a cement-plastered mud house, with the cement cracked so badly, more of the mud is obvious.

Mam, a pregnant woman whose age could be anything between twenty and fifty, comes out of the house and looks about in search of her 12-year old daughter, Undeana. She wears a blouse and wrapper tied over her chest with an unmatched scarf.

Ezor walks to the mud house and Mam greets him pleasantly.

"I was just about to call Undeana to come and find you," Mam says and cups her hand over her mouth. "Undeana!" She looks to the sides of the mud house. "Undeana."

"Mam!" Undeana runs in panting. "My mother."

Sweat pours from Undeana's thick hair into her face making her look less fair than she really is. She's a pretty girl with attractive eyes, high cheek bones, and a beautiful smile.

Mam is not moved by the girl's enthusiasm. "Where went you?"

Undeana takes in air through her mouth. "I went to check on my chicks."

Mam smirks. "Hmmm. Undeana! Come on, go and prepare dinner. It's getting late."

Undeana's joy overpowers the antagonism. "Mam, if you see how big my chicks are now. Papa for like am well well."

"Come on, go inside."

Undeana shrugs. "Mam, you'll see." She laughs. "Broda Ezor, una welcome o." She runs inside.

Ezor shakes his head. "She's big now."

"And just a bundle of activity. I don't know what to do with her."

Mam removes a chewing stick from somewhere in her blouse, and chews on it. You, you no go sidon? No vex; I no get nothing to give you o..." She lowers herself to a small wooden stool.

Ezor pulls another stool close and sits. "If na money you dey find."

"The problem too much. All these children, no husband, no money."

"Give Undeana for money woman na."

Mam screams. "Ah, Ezor."

Ezor shrugs. "No be you dey find money? Even dis one wey you carry for belle sef. No be wahala all don join?"

Mam shifts her stool to put distance between them. "Wetin be your problem, Ezor, devil."

Ezor sneers. "Na hin be my problem. No be help I dey find give you?"

Mam licks her lips. "How much?"

Ezor giggles. "2,5."

Mam throws her hands up in the air. "Na tif you be, Ezor. Comot here."

Ezor stands. "Hunger go soon kill you." He looks round. "Person wey get bush meat for backyard dey beg for dead rat?"

Mam sighs. "I dey go me de oder side for Cameroon. My late husband friend wan make I waka come. Weda he go find me small money."

Ezor smiles. "How much be ya trans?"

Mam bites her lower lip. "7." If only Ezor was a little generous. She hopes he has changed, but can a leopard change its skin?

Ezor laughs and throws his head back. "I go give you 5. For Undeana."

Mam gasps. Oh, the evil Ezor can never change. "Na 10. No be I go chop, waka go market, buy food for these small children?"

Ezor straightens his thick bulk. "I dey go see Cholufor. After I go come see you, make we talk am final."

Mam hates him but he had always been close when all the other members of her late husband abandoned her. His closeness may not have done her much good in life but at least, he was there.

Mam stands too. "10 o. I no go take 5 o."

Ezor walks away, laughing.

—

Undeana walks out to Mam, carrying her three-year-old brother, Agona who wears only a dirty pant and has tear-streaks on his chubby cheeks. His stomach is bulky, and his arms are thin.

Undeana looks at Mam. "Mam, wetin dat wicked Ezor find come here?"

Mam rolls her eyes. "Wetin concern you, Undeana. Una too dey ask question."

Undeana frowns. "Ah Mam. You know say Ezor papa na hin kill my papa. Just so that they can take his farm."

Mam shakes her head. "Ezor na ya broda. No talk like dat. If no be for Ezor, how we for dey survive?"

Undeana is not moved. She balances Agona on her hip. "Wetin Ezor wan sell give you now. Or na buy e wan buy?"

Mam hisses. "Shut ya mouth, Undeana. Dat small school wey you just go small, na hin wan turn your head. Go fetch water."

Undeana is undaunted. She plans to know what Ezor came to do in their house. Ezor lives in Calabar and behaves like a big man every time he visits the village but never has he bought anything for her or Mam. Undeana hated him with a passion.

"I don fetch finish."

Mam looks at her. "You don wash cloth finish?"

"I don finish am."

Mam tries harder. "Wey ya oda sister and broda? Dem don chop?"

Undeana lowers her voice to hide her irritation. Her mother does this when she has something to hide.

"Dem don chop."

Mam says, "Go inside. I wan go see Ebiya."

Undeana is alarmed. "You still dey owe am? Mam, wetin you no wan tell me?"

"Go inside."

Undeana stamps her feet and shifts Agona in her arm. The boy is getting too big suddenly. "Wetin Ezor come talk?"

Mam rises to her feet and walks on to the village path. Undeana remains standing, looking after her mother's receding figure. Her sisters, eight-year-old Ayam and ten-year-old Metesh walk out to her. She herds them back into the hut.

—

Cholufor, a wrinkled old dark-skinned man is seated on a rafter rocker in front of a cement bungalow, chewing snuff leaf. The sun has set and left only a cool beginning to the evening. Cholufor's favourite time of day to relax and entertain guests.

Ezor walks into the compound, beaming. "Cholufor! The only millionaire in Cameroon and Nigeria."

Cholufor snickers. "Ezor, the only evil man in Becheve Kingdom. *Wejend o!* Wetin carry you come dis time?"

Ezor laughs. "Ahaha! Cholufor, wise old man. You always know what to say."

Ezor takes a seat though he isn't offered one.

"Will you take snuff with me?" Cholufor picks a small bottle from the ground beside him.

Ezor laughs. "I cannot resist the offer of a rich man. They say your snuff is the strongest this side of river Niger."

Cholufor raises his voice. "Okong!"

Okong's deep voice rises from within the house. "Papa!"

"Bring snuff for Ezor, the great traveller."

"Yes papa."

Cholufor turns to Ezor. "How is our great state capital? What are the politicians doing with our wealth?"

"Eating us black. Ripping us into pieces," Ezor says.

Cholufor grunts. "Make sure you eat your part of the national cake very well."

Okong, an able-bodied young man in his mid-twenties, walks out of the house with the snuff and serves Ezor without greeting him.

Ezor takes the snuff. "Did your manners go on a journey, Okong? Have you not seen me?"

Cholufor waves at Okong. "Greet Ezor or he will take his goodwill away."

Okong extends a hand to Ezor. "Good evening, Ezor, the great traveller."

Cholufor takes a sniff. "These days Ezor no longer lives in Calabar but goes to Abuja.

Okong's slight frame betrays his big voice. "Good for him." He walks back into the house.

Ezor gasps. "If not for you, Cholufor, I will get boys to teach Okong some manners."

Cholufor snickers. "He will learn."

Ezor sniffs. "Ah, I am not surprised. I must take some of this to Calabar. The boys will pay anything for this good thing."

Cholufor frowns. "You have still not stated your matter, Ezor. You do not see masquerades in the morning time without a reason."

Ezor puts the snuff on the ground carefully. "Cholufor, I go back in two days. But before I leave, I have a big proposal to make."

CHAPTER THREE

PRESENT DAY

Rose is seated at her reading table in a room for two in the University of Calabar medical students' hostel. There is an open textbook in front of her with an open notebook and pencil. She stares into space and there are unshed tears in her eyes.

Yaya's voice from outside the room jolts her. "Roseline! Rose!"

Rose quickly cleans her eyes. Yaya, her bubbly, beautiful roommate would pry the truth from her if she notices the tears and Rose is not up to the task.

"Yes?" Rose turns to the door.

Yaya bursts in and swoons. "You can't believe who I met today, Rose." She drops her bag on her bed.

Rose arches her eyebrow. "Michelle Obama."

Yaya laughs. "Ohhh o Rose. You're very funny. It's not only Michelle. It's Queen of England."

Rose smiles. "With all this noise, it has to be one very important person."

Yaya purses her lips. "Sunny Neji."

Rose shrugs. "Uhn? Who is that?"

Yaya throws her hands on her head and drops on her bed. "Ah, my life! Rose, you don't even rock one bit. Sunny Neji. 2Face's second. When it's only reading you know. All is book book book."

Rose smirks. "Do I even know 2Face?"

Yaya's eyes widen in shock and Rose bursts into laughter. "Cool down. I am only joking."

Yaya sighs. "Naughty girl."

Rose folds her arms. "So, where did you see Sunny Neji. On campus or in town?" She knows Yaya will be full of some wonderful story, so she leans back on her chair.

"You won't believe it. In the hospital."

Rose sits up, showing more interest. "Ahha, what did he come for? Was he sick?"

Yaya smiles. "Apparently, he and CMD's son are friends. He came to check on him."

"Interesting. You mean he came all the way from Lagos just for a visit? Isn't he lucky?"

"But do you know Sunny Neji is also from Cross River?"

Rose doesn't know. "Really? That's interesting. I thought he was from Lagos. With that popular song he sang in Yoruba."

Yaya nods. "Eh, you know all these artistes. They are very versatile. He may have lived in Lagos for long too."

"Hmm."

"See, I was so star-struck, Dr. Ashi was just laughing at me." Yaya looks at Rose with a frown. "Do you even know Dr. Ashi? He's a fine bloke too."

Rose thinks of Dr. Ashi and his first meeting with her and decides not to tell her best friend and roommate, Yaya. It is best left disregarded.

The following day, Rose walks purposefully along the corridor of the hospital, her lab coat hung loosely on her shoulder, carrying a folder. Dr. Ashi appears behind her and walks fast to catch up with her.

"Rose!"

Rose stops. "Ah, Dr. Ashi." She curtseys. "Good afternoon sir."

Ashi frowns. "Are you trying to embarrass me? I asked you to stop curtseying for me and call me Ashi."

Rose doesn't mean to be stubborn or rude. Involuntarily, she curtseys again. "I'm sorry sir."

Ashi squeezes his face in anger. "I don't find it funny, Rose."

Rose looks away unable to engage his intense gaze. "I'm not used to this. You're my boss."

"But I told you. I don't want to be your boss. I want more."

Rose shakes her head. "But it's not possible. You're too far ahead of me."

Ashi clenches his jaw. "How? How am I too far ahead of you? Why don't you leave that for me to decide?"

Rose steals a glance at Ashi. "Dr. Ashi..."

"Ashi."

Rose shakes her head. Ashi touches her arm lightly. "You are even avoiding me. Why? Am I that horrible for you?" he says.

Rose steps back. "Ashi. You're too far from me. I'm not in your class—"

Before she would embarrass herself and burst into tears, Rose turns and hurries away.

CHAPTER FOUR

M am rushes to the house and at the entrance, raises her voice. "Undeana! Make una come o."

Undeana walks out of the house leisurely. She stretches. "Mam."

Mam is breathless. "Undeana."

Undeana yawns. She wonders what Mam is up to now. Who is chasing her from where she went? "Mam. Una welcome o."

Mam doesn't give away her exasperation. Undeana has found out her mother shows little emotion many times. After her father died when she was just seven, Mam has been with at least three men, hoping each would marry her. She's had Agona for one of them and now she's pregnant again to only she knows.

"Undeana! How many times did I call you?"

Undeana nearly rolls her eyes. "Mam, three times. Wetin happen?"

Mam does a little dance that surprises Undeana. Mam can be dramatic at times. "Ezor wan carry you go Calabar."

Undeana jumps back as though stung. "Hey! The gods of heaven rejects it."

Mam stops her drama. "Calm down, child."

Undeana grumbles and a shudder runs through her body. "God forbid bad thing. Mam, Ezor is wicked. Just like his name says. My destiny rejects it. I knew he was up to some evil when he came."

Mam bares her teeth in a soulless smile. Undeana can count the number of times she's seen her mother smile.

"That's what I first said. But Ezor said he's taking you back to school."

Undeana widens her eyes. "Hey? School in Calabar?"

Mam chuckles. "Yes. Calabar."

Undeana feels conflicted. This is what she has always wanted; to go to school. But... "Ah, Mam! What, how, what do they do in Calabar that I know?"

Mam laughs. "You'll have to learn their ways."

"Ah. Calabar." Undeana lowers her voice, unsure. "But, Mam. I want to go to school. But what if Ezor—how will he—what will I have to do for him?"

Mam brightens up. "Undeana! Is he not your cousin? Can he not do something for our family?" Mam claps. "Ezor said he will send you to school. And he will."

Undeana screams and jumps up and starts to dance. "Ezor said he'll send me to school. Ezor said he will send me to school."

Mam laughs loud.

Early the following morning, Undeana packs her load, tied in a scarf, and balances it on her head. Mam comes to her side and folds some money into her hand. She quickly tucks it into her wrapper. Undeana curtseys.

Ezor approaches. "Good morning."

Mam has tears in her eyes. "Don't forget home."

Undeana is overwhelmed. She clenches her teeth to keep from crying. "I won't forget home, my mother." She looks at her mother and sniffs. "My mother. Please look after my chicks for me."

Ezor snickers. "Goodbye." He turns to the road and Undeana follows him.

Undeana cries huge tears, and heaves. Ezor walks in front, indifferent. Mam follows them waving.

The journey is a long one. Ezor and Undeana walk through the village path. They walk amidst the thick bush path and get to a small stream which they cross. Undeana pauses several times but continues to follow Ezor.

It is a long journey and Undeana keeps thinking they should soon get to the main road where they will get a bus to Calabar. Surely Ezor cannot think they will walk all the way to Calabar but Undeana has never left Kundeve and the neighbouring villages. She knows buses come and go to the big cities like Calabar, but she has no clue how far away it is.

Ezor gives her some food at some point and they stop to rest twice.

Finally, Ezor and Undeana approach a small village. Unlike how they've done in other villages, Ezor stops to greet some people and walk to a bungalow. The house looks like the biggest and the finest in the village. Undeana thinks it belongs to the village head.

She taps Ezor. "Na where be dis?"

Ezor squares his shoulders. "Dis na Cholufor house."

Undeana looks around. "No be Calabar be dis."

Ezor laughs hard. "Village girl."

They reach the bungalow. Undeana pulls at Ezor's cloth. "Who be Cholufor? Where be dis?"

Ezor turns on her. "Na where your mami tell you say you dey go?"

Undeana frowns. "Calabar. She say you tell am say you wan carry me go school."

Ezor kicks the dust and laughs. "Ewo! School kwa. Na here wey I tell your mama say I dey bring you."

Undeana shudders. "Na where be dis eh!"

Ezor waves his hands in the air around her. "I bring you for ya husband im house. Na Cholufor house. Cholufor don give me ten thousand naira for your mother."

CHAPTER FIVE

Undeana, carries her scarf of clothes and runs wildly through the bush path, weeping and sweating, turning to look over her shoulders. She falls once, and rises, running. Two men jump out of the bush and grab her. She struggles viciously...

Rose turns and tosses on her bed. She struggles a bit then wakes up with a start. She sweats profusely. She sits up slowly and looks at Yaya who is fast asleep on the other bed. Rose swallows, and mops sweat from her forehead. She slowly lay back, but her eyes are wide open.

—

Dr. Ashi and his handsome colleague and friend, Abai are in the doctor's room. They catch a glimpse through the partially opened curtain, of Rose across the hall, helping a mother carry her sick baby, and walk out of sight.

Ashi shakes his head. "I've never seen a girl so
stubborn."

Abai arches his eyebrow. "What's her problem?"

Ashi shrugs. "It amazes me. She's even avoiding me these days."

Abai laughs. "Means you're choking her."

"I can't even concentrate. I just keep seeing her everywhere," Ashi
says.

Abai laughs. "These girls. They can make one go crazy."

"Which man will not like this girl? She's just so sweet. And she has good character too."

"Or does she have a husband?"

Ashi gasps. "No way. She doesn't wear a ring."

Abai shrugs. "That means nothing these days."

Meanwhile on the other side of the hospital, Rose, wearing a lab coat, talks to the baby's mother in the paediatric ward, while carrying the baby.

She looks at the mother of the baby. "Hmm, God saved you. Never use hot water to bath a baby when she has fever. It can kill the baby. Instead use lukewarm water or dip a towel into cool water to mop the body. God forbid bad thing."

The mother looks uneasy for a moment. "When I tried cold water, she screamed."

Rose shakes her head. "It doesn't mean. If you follow these children, they'll die before you know it. God forbid." She nuzzles the child and the baby giggles. "Don't be sick o, sweet baby."

Dr. Ashi walks straight to where she is, with a smile on his face. "Wife, how are you? Thanks for not asking after me."

Rose hands over the baby to the mother and moves away from her. "You too thanks for traveling without telling us."

Ashi laughs. They walk toward the exit. "I want to see you."

Rose shrugs. "I'm here."

Ashi looks at her. "Over dinner."

Rose stops short and sighs heavily. "Dr. Ashi. I told you it can't work."

Ashi moves out of the way for someone to pass. "Says who?"

Rose shakes her head. "I'm not up to your class."

Ashi frowns. "Says who?"

"Dr. Ashi..."

"Ashi."

Rose sighs. What more could she say? She pleads with her eyes, but he looks so resolved, her heart thuds. He's been on her neck about this for over a month continuously. What will she do?

"I'll pick you up for 6. Should we go and eat fresh fish? Point and kill?" He gives her his most disarming smile. "Hmm?"

Rose shakes her head. But Ashi doesn't seem to notice her protest.

"Do you stay in medical students' hostel?" Rose nods. "Then?" Rose shakes her head. "See you."

He walks away without waiting for her response. Rose hugs her arms to herself and sighs.

CHAPTER SIX

U ndeana gasps at Ezor's statement. Money woman! Ah! Mam sold her? She looks round, seeking escape but how? The house is big so the owner must be rich. He may be the richest man in the whole village. Everyone will know her. They will chase her. Ezor will not even let her run now.

Undeana opens her mouth to reply but an old man walks out of the house. His hair is low but looks shaggy and grey. He is tall, and bulky with a round belly. He looks different from the normal village people, cleaner. He wears a shirt and ties the traditional wrapper. Undeana wonders if this is the Cholufor, her new owner.

He walks up to them and Ezor beams at him. "Ah, Cholufor the richest man on earth. I greet you."

Cholufor throws a careless glance at her. "You have come with your cunny."

Undeana moves to stand behind Ezor, trembling.

Ezor gives a mock bow. "I have brought your wife."

Cholufor sits on a solid cane rocking chair. "Good. I would send dogs after you if you did not."

Ezor raises his hands. "A retired soldier like you? I dare not."

Cholufor looks at Undeana again, this time, assessing. "Undeana, or what is your name?"

"Undeana," Ezor says.

"Come here. Let me see if you are worth twenty thousand," Cholufor says.

"Hahaha, the great Cholufor. You will see. She will surpass all the others you have. She works like a horse." He pushes Undeana forward. "Show your face."

"Hmm." Cholufor raises his voice. "Okong!"

Okong responds from within the house. "Papa."

"Come and take Undeana inside."

Okong walks in. "Una welcome o." He looks at Undeana suggestively.

Cholufor waves his index finger at him. "If you touch this one, Okong."

Okong grins. "Come Undeana."

Undeana reluctantly follows him with a look of feeling betrayed on her face. She tries to make eye contact with Ezor but he ignores her and instead makes small talk with Cholufor.

Inside the house is stuffy and dark and big. Okong walks through as though he has cat eyes and can see in the dark, right through a long corridor. There is a door at the end of the spacious corridor, and it opens to a courtyard. Undeana notices movement but Okong opens the last door to the right just before the courtyard.

Undeana follows him in. The room is semi-dark and a small fire burns from a clay gourd.

"You will use this room now," Okong says. "But when your husband comes, he will give you your own room."

He steps out and Undeana falls to her knees and weeps

silently. She knows exactly what this means. She will never go to school in her life. She will never be free again. Oh, Mam, why? Why?

Tired and exhausted from the journey, Undeana falls asleep on a mat on the floor. She only startles awake when a hand pats her bottom. She jumps and scoots away from the intruder.

A gruff voice says, "It's me, don't be afraid."

"Please leave me alone."

Cholufor chuckles. "You talk to your owner like that? Do you want me to flog you?"

Undeana takes more steps away from him and her back hits the cool wall.

"Remove your clothes," Cholufor says dryly.

Undeana shakes her head. "No, please. Please, God will bless you."

Impatiently, the old man closes up on her and pulls her wrapper off, and then pulls at her dress, shoving it over her head, and to the floor. Undeana picks up her wrapper. Cholufor struggles to take it from her but Undeana pushes him with all her strength.

She runs out of the house clutching a wrapper to her chest, weeping. She doesn't know where to go but she just needs to get away from him. The house is quiet and everywhere is dark. It must be very late.

Cholufor follows her out slowly, bare-chested with only his wrapper tied to his waist. "Come here, Undeana."

Undeana falls to her knees. "Please Cholufor. I beg you." She has heard many stories of how men cause pain for girls her age, and those younger all in the name of money marriage. She still can't believe Mam sold her and lied to her. Ah. Which is easier to accept? Selling her or lying about going to school?

Cholufor's voice remains calm. "I don't have the time or the power to chase you. Come inside."

Undeana sobs. "I want to die. I want to die..."

Cholufor raises his voice. "Okong!"

Undeana's heart lurches. She fears the young man she just met earlier. He didn't say much but the look in his eyes sent terror to her heart. No, she'd rather the old man handle her. She runs back into the house.

Cholufor follows her in.

In the interior darkness of Cholufor's room, rustles of clothing is heard, and then the moans of Cholufor, followed by Undeana's wails, which rent the silence of the night.

CHAPTER SEVEN

Dawn breaks over the village of Imale II and Cholufor's compound awakes. Women and children walk in and out of the house going about their chores. There is no sign of Undeana.

Cholufor comes out of the house and stands in the middle of the compound and raises his voice. "Undeana!"

There is no response and he calls again. "Undeana!"

Okong walks out to Cholufor. "Her clothes are not in the room."

Cholufor gasps. "Take Suffer with you. Go and find her."

—

Undeana fast-walks through the village path dressed in her blouse and wrapper. She clutches her scarf of clothes to her chest and makes as much haste as the pain between her legs will let her. She never imagined such pain existed. Her heart thuds as she meets women going to the stream, but no one stops her. She continues through the bush till she meets no one.

The sun rises high up, and Undeana walks tiredly along the bush path till she comes to a stream. She runs to the stream and takes a drink. She washes her face and sits on the bank, looking around and panting. She begins to talk to herself. She doesn't even know the name of Cholufor's village, but she knows Kundeve. She prays she will meet someone who will tell her which way to take to Kundeve.

But she doesn't even want to go back to Mam. If she does, they will only return her to Cholufor. But where else can she go? She's estranged from her father's family and she really doesn't know many people in her mother's family. They are a poor family, and everyone has their own problems.

She remembers the money Mam gave her. Maybe she can go somewhere else nobody knows her and settle down with the money. She unties the edge of her scarf and takes out the money. It should be enough to... ten naira. She gasps and bites her lower lip. Mam gave her only ten naira?! Anger rises in her belly like a great fish from the river.

There is a disturbance in the nearby bush. Undeana catches sight of Okong and a retarded sort of man, just moments before they burst out of the bush. Undeana grabs her scarf and makes a run but the two men catch her and drag her away with them.

They are rough with her as she imagined Okong would be but they did not beat her. The walk back to the village is quicker than she expects, and she wonders if she ever left the village at all. Of course, she doesn't know the way so she may have only walked deeper into the lands instead of away.

They walk into the compound. Cholufor is seated on his normal rocker, eating. A young woman is seated beside him, carrying a baby. Okong pushes Undeana and she falls to her knees in front of Cholufor.

Okong heaves, his muscled chest twitch. "You try and run away again, I will tie you up on the evil tree, and allow the gods to eat you."

Cholufor nods. "Thank you, Okong. And Suffer."

Okong and Suffer exit. Cholufor continues to eat and ignores Undeana. When he finishes, he enters the house.

The young woman stares at Undeana for a while and rocks her baby. "You must never run away again."

Undeana breathes heavily. "I will continue to run till the day I die."

"My name is Caro." Then she smiles. "Your day to die is near then. Is it not better to take the fate the gods have given you? Have children and live?"

Undeana sits on the ground. "I don't want children who will end up like me."

Caro shakes her head. She seems to be in a world of her own. "I remember last year when our husband bought Azagha. Her father said she was bad luck. Nobody wanted her. Cholufor was generous to even agree to buy her. She ran away the same way you did. After the first night."

Caro describes explicitly how a teenage girl runs wildly through the bush path, weeping and sweating, turning to look over her shoulders. She falls once, and rises, running. Okong and Suffer jump out of the bush and grab her. They drag her struggling viciously to the trunk of a banana tree and tie her to it. And walk back the way they came, cursing at her and snapping their fingers.

Caro rocks her baby. "They did not return with Azagha. Many tales followed this. Some said the gods ate her up. Some said the evil tree swallowed her. Some said she must have died of hunger, tied to the tree like that."

Undeana swallows hard. "What did Cholufor do?"

Caro smiles. "Nothing. What can he do? Azagha ran away. It is a taboo to run."

Undeana shrugs. "I don't care. I will not allow that dirty old man to touch me again."

Caro smirks. "Before you run, imagine yourself alone in the forest tied to a tree. I will rather have all of them touch me, than die like that." She gets to her feet.

Undeana thinks of making her a friend. She needs someone badly. "When did you come here?"

Caro looks at her. "Two years ago. I did not even have breast."

Undeana blinks back tears. "My mother tricked me. She said I was going to school."

Caro's voice is flat. "Hmm. My father was owing Cholufor three thousand. He agreed to take me and give my father five thousand to balance." She begins to walk into the house.

Undeana rises to her feet. "Please. I'm hungry. I've not eaten today."

Caro chuckles. "I will give you food but, in the morning, you must ask Cholufor for a small piece of land, and farm for your own food."

Undeana gasps. "But anything I farm cannot grow overnight?"

Caro narrows her eyes. "Suffer is generous and kind. If you do anything he asks."

She walks away, and Undeana ponders on what that could mean.

CHAPTER EIGHT

Undeana wakes up with all the others in Cholufor's household, carries a basket with hoe and cutlass, and walks through the bush path to a small farm. Other women and children are on the farm too. She drops her basket and begins to hoe a small portion. Caro is seen across the farm, her baby is laid on the grass, sleeping.

She had pondered on Caro's words, and decided to buy time. She would endure all the abuse till she has some money and knows her way around. Then they will never see her again.

With dusk approaching, Undeana walks into the compound with her basket. Cholufor is seated on his rafter chair with some village guests, smoking pipe.

Undeana mumbles, "Una well done o."

The visitors mumble responses. Cholufor says,

"Welcome."

There is a disturbance from within the house. Two women's voices are heard. There is the sound of beating and slapping. Undeana runs out of the house tying only wrapper.

Cholufor glares at her. "What is the matter now? Can you not see we have visitors?"

Undeana pants. "I no tif meat from Uteye's pot. She say I take her meat."

Uteye, a woman in her early thirties rushes out of the house. "Wey she dey get meat from?"

Undeana says, "I dey get my meat."

Uteye claps. "From where? Tif!!"

Cholufor growls. "Leave this place now, both of you before I curse you!"

Undeana needs to defend herself. She can't let the saucy Uteye have a final say. "Suffer dey give me meat!"

Cholufor jumps from his seat. "I say leave now!"

Uteye and Undeana go back inside. Sounds of loud slaps and Uteye's voice cursing is heard and Undeana's cries and denial.

Undeana goes out of the house long after everyone has turned in, a habit she finds consoling. She sits alone outside looking at the stars. Suffer comes out of the house. He walks over to her and begins to rub her back.

Undeana prefers to be alone. "Suffer stop it." She flinches.

Suffer behaves like a child and Undeana has often wondered at him. He must be retarded or has the sense of a child. But Undeana finds him engaging, and like Caro suggested, he is kind and understanding. Perhaps the only kind person in Cholufor's household.

Suffer grunts. "Why? After eating almost one full bush meat."

Undeana shifts from his touch. "I gave you what you want."

After the attack from Uteye earlier, Undeana really just wants to be alone. Her plan to run away is still alive in her but she doesn't want to be caught a second time. She has to plan it properly the next time.

Suffer touches her thick hair. "I like you. Don't you want meat again?"

Undeana shrugs him off. "No. Uteye will say it is her meat."

Suffer moans. "Uteye is a fool."

Undeana doesn't want to hear more. She wants to be left alone. "I don't care."

Suffer pulls her to him. "I will give you two bush meat that I dry myself."

Undeana hates his touch and he drools on her whenever she sleeps in his room. "No, Suffer. I don't want again."

Suffer sulks. "What will you eat?"

Undeana shrugs. "My cassava is almost ready. I will sell it."

Suffer grumbles. "Papa said you have to start cooking for him. You are very lucky he even allowed you to wait small. Caro cooked the following day after she came."

Undeana had discovered to her shock that Okong and Suffer were brothers though from different mothers. No one ever talks about their mothers though.

"That is Caro. Not me."

Suffer caresses her cheek. "Please now."

"No. Don't touch me, Suffer."

"Please. I like—"

Okong walks out and sees them. Undeana moves away from Suffer and hugs her body.

Okong walks over to her and looks at her in a seductive way. "Your romance with Suffer will soon be over." He frowns. "Papa wants you."

Undeana stands to her feet. She has learnt early not to disobey commands.

Okong looks at Suffer. "What do you give her that I cannot?"

Suffer smiles foolishly. "Ask her."

Undeana runs into the house, annoyed.

CHAPTER NINE

Undeana rushes out of the house to a nearby bush and begins to throw up. She stays there for a while, trying to get her bearing. Uteye comes out of the house and walks slowly to her, hissing and clapping.

"So, who is the owner of this one since it is Okong today and Suffer tomorrow?"

Her query meets with silence. Undeana continues to bend over the bush.

Uteye continues. "They say these girls are small, but they know more than their mothers." She nudges Undeana with her feet. "Am I not talking to you?"

Another bout of nausea takes over Undeana, and she continues to empty her stomach in the bush. She really wishes she will understand what is happening to her because she doesn't get sick easily.

"When the bastard comes out, we will see whose head it resembles." Uteye hisses and walks away. She meets Caro, who is carrying a bowl of water, on the way and they exchange mean looks. Uteye goes inside the house. Caro goes to Undeana.

"Don't allow Uteye to get at you," Caro says and gives Undeana the bowl of water.

"I will try." Undeana rinses her mouth. "What does she mean by that?"

Caro shrugs. "Jealousy is her problem."

Undeana pours the rest of the water on her head. "Did Cholufor buy her too?"

"No. She did love marriage with him."

Undeana sighs. "Isn't she lucky?"

Caro hisses. "Is she? How is she better than us?"

Undeana gasps. "Because Cholufor loves her. He takes care of her."

Caro grunts. "Sometimes."

Undeana rolls her eyes. "I wish I will marry someone for love."

Caro chuckles. "You're still a child. When you grow older there will be no difference."

Undeana eyes her. "You're not too much older than me."

Caro pouts. "I am sixteen. How old are you?"

"My mother says I am fourteen, but I think I am twelve."

"So, we can just call you thirteen. You're still a child."

"Not now."

"Hmm." Caro collects her bowl. "Take care of yourself. I lost my first baby to Uteye's kicks." She walks back into the house.

Undeana stares after her.

Undeana gets used to the abuses, the early morning nausea, and working to earn a living for herself. She goes to the farm, cooks for Cholufor when it is her turn to do so, sleep with Cholufor whenever he calls for her, and notice the changes in her body. Her life is hard, and she only takes it one day at a time.

Nothing happening to her seem strange to the others. She sometimes thinks about her mother. Would Mam have had her new baby by now? Nobody brings any news from Kundeve. From living with her mother, she knows a lot about pregnancy. She doesn't know how else she would cope. No one tells anybody anything. Not even Caro.

One day, Undeana returns from the farm with products. Her stomach is very big. At the entrance of the house, she bends and gives a loud shout. Women and children run to her aid. They rush her inside. Undeana's labour wails is heard far out in the village.

The baby finally comes out several hours later, but it refuses to cry. The village midwife, an old bent woman who is famed to have delivered more than half of the villagers, does all her tricks but the baby doesn't cry.

The woman throws the baby in the air several times. After almost half an hour of pouring water over the baby, she wraps the baby in Undeana's cloth and tells the household the gods have taken the baby back. Shouts of wailing and sadness is heard in the dead of the night.

—

Undeana is seated on a low stool, washing clothes. Caro walks to her, heavily pregnant.

"I left clothes for you to help me wash. You did not carry it."

Undeana pauses. "I did not see it."

Caro keeps her arms akimbo. "How did you not see it? After all the help I have given you in this compound. Is it my fault your baby died? When you were lying for Okong and Suffer and Cholufor, how will the gods not take the baby whose father you don't know?"

Undeana drops the cloth in her hand. "Aha, Caro. Why are you talking to me like this? I said I did not see your clothes."

Caro raises her voice. "You lie. Uteye said it. You are just a wicked little liar."

Undeana hisses. "Caro, if the pain of your baby is coming, say it. Not to be cursing me like this early in the morning."

Caro smirks. "You are jealous. I did not kill your baby and you cannot kill mine."

Undeana closes her eyes for a moment. She is glad the baby died. She doesn't want such a child. It's true she doesn't even know the father, but she dares not say any of this or they will say she killed her baby and tie her to the evil tree and leave her to be eaten by wild animals in the forest.

"God forbid that your baby die," Undeana mutters.

Caro says, "Of course. My baby has one father. He cannot die."

Undeana looks at her hand. "My baby too had one father. I never did this thing—like that with Suffer or Okong. It was the midwife who choked my baby."

Caro turns on her and begins to walk off. "Save your explanation for the oracle."

Undeana stares after her with tears gathered in her eyes.

CHAPTER TEN

Ezor walks into Kundeve village as the sun sets. None of the children around run to greet him. He walks cautiously till he gets to his house, and slips in. His mother makes some noise inside and raises her voice.

"Who is it?"

Ezor meets her on the corridor. "Mama, it's me. Don't shout."

His mother jumps on him. "Ezor!!!"

They walk into a small parlour with three wooden chairs. Ezor's father comes in to join them.

Mama Ezor does a little dance and sits. "What did you bring for us? How's your wife?"

Ezor frowns. "I didn't bring anything. I hear Undeana's mother died."

Mama Ezor exchanges glances with her husband. "No.

She died? We did not hear any such thing. She only told us

she was going to Cameroon with her children. She said Undeana ran away."

Papa Ezor shrugs. "I still saw her three days ago. You should check on her."

Ezor slumps into a seat. "Things have not been easy. I have a serious police case. No one must know I am here."

Papa Ezor sits straight and exclaims along with his wife. "You know our village is a small one. Everyone knows everyone. What did you do to police?"

"I beat hell out of one foolish woman for cheating me before she confessed. Even her husband saw her and couldn't recognize her," Ezor said.

Mama Ezor gasps. "You beat another man's wife?"

"To rags, mama."

Mama Ezor opens her mouth, horrified. "Ah. What if the police come here?"

"You know how people talk." Papa Ezor frowns. "Do you have friends who know where you are from?"

Ezor sniffs. "Of course, I am a businessman in Calabar."

Papa Ezor turns to Ezor. "You cannot stay here. You have to leave."

Mama Ezor cries. "Where will he go?"

Amidst tears and pleading from his mother, Ezor walks out of his house into the village path with his bag. His mother follows him weeping, and then turns back. Ezor continues on the path, murmuring to himself. Three men jump on him and beat him up. They take his bag and run back into the bush.

Ezor limps to the front of Mam's house. His clothes are dirty and torn. Dawn is just breaking, and he is grateful to be alive after the assault of the night.

"Mam Undeana! Una don wake? How una sleep?"

Mam answers from within the house. "Ezor, you come? You come na for wetin?"

Ezor sits on the floor. "I wan see you."

Mam walks out tied in wrapper and carrying a baby

about six months old. "Hope no problem."

Ezor looks at her. "How for Undeana?"

Mam shrugs. "No. Wetin?"

Ezor gasps for air. "I hear say she die."

"Die?" Bites her lower tongue. "I no hear."

Ezor breathes heavily. "Cholufor don dey find me come Calabar. Say make I replace Undeana. As I no hear from you, I no believe. But as I go yesterday, see beating Okong his son gi me."

Mam sighs. "Na wa o. So, Undeana die, and no man no fit come for dis wa place to even tell me? Choi! Di kin suffer wey person don see for dis life?"

Ezor sighs. "You sabi how we dey do tins for country talk; na Metesh I com carry."

Mam exclaims. "You come carry for wetin?"

"You know our custom. Your daughter never reach one year for man house before she, she die; you go gi anoda woman pikin."

Mam frowns. "Metesh na only ten years. How you wan make she marry man?"

"See, no be me do the culture and you know. No be me send you to give your daughter for money marriage. Na culture. Or I go report you to the elders." Ezor groans. "Give me water first. And food."

Mam hesitates and then stand to do his bidding.

Ezor closes his eyes and moans. When Mam doesn't return on time, he raises his voice. "Be fast abeg." He slowly spreads himself on the ground, flinching several times as pain courses through his body.

Mam returns with food and water. "Please Ezor. Metesh never ripe enough. Na only ten years she be."

Ezor digs into the food and doesn't respond for a while. "I don arrange money woman for eight years. Go prepare her. When I finish eating and rest small, I dey take her go Cholufor."

Mam flexes her fingers. "But wetin kill my daughter sef? How she take die wey you go wan come take anoda one?"

"Na your business be dat?"

"How my pikin take die you say no be—"

"Hmm. See na Cholufor money you still dey chop so. You must replace ya daughter for hin house." Ezor belches. "Na when she dey try born pikin she die."

Mam takes deep breathes but says nothing more. She returns into the house and wakes Metesh. Within the hour, Metesh walks out of the house and bids her mother farewell amidst tears.

Ezor walks through the village bush path. Metesh carries her load tied up in a scarf and follows behind him.

Several hours later, they walk into Ugbakoko, a small village with many mud huts, and stop in front of a cement-plastered mud hut.

Ezor raises his voice. "I dey greet."

An old man walks out. "Ah Ezor the traveller. Una welcome o."

Ezor yawns. "Thank you, Oliaza. I don come from far. Give me water, please."

Oliaza raises his voice. "Bring water."

A girl about Metesh's age brings water for Ezor.

Ezor drinks. "I don bring ya woman. Oyibo call am insurance pol-icy."

Oliaza smiles and bares blackened teeth. "Good." He looks at Metesh. "This one small o."

Ezor chuckles. "Woman na woman."

Oliaza assesses Metesh, and nods. "Hmmm. Wetin be her name?"

"Metesh."

"Hmm, okay." Oliaza looks at Metesh. "Go wait me inside."

Metesh looks at Ezor who waves her inside. She enters the house.

Ezor lowers his voice. "Na ten thousand plus all de small small tins dem wey you go do for him mami. You, you sabi nor!"

"Hahaha, the traveller." Oliaza dips his hand in his pocket. "Ten thousand."

Ezor collects the money and keeps it. "Thank you. Take care of her o. Na my cousin."

Oliaza chuckles. "You hear me no dey care for dem?"

"I hope so." Ezor stretches and rises. "I dey go."

Oliaza waves at him. "Make you waka fine."

CHAPTER ELEVEN

Yaya lounges on her bed, reading a novel. Rose walks in, mumbles a greeting, and walks to her bed. She removes her shoes, lay on her bed, and closes her eyes.

Yaya sits up and stares at Rose's melancholic behaviour. "Hope nothing?"

Rose sighs and sits up to face Yaya. "Dr. Ashi wants to take me out."

Yaya jumps up and goes to hug Rose. "Hey!!! My friend don hammer."

Rose bursts into tears. Yaya leaps to her side. "Aha. What's wrong?"

Rose shakes her head. "I'm not in his class. People like him don't date people like me." She sobs. "If he knows my story, he'll throw me away like dirty water."

Yaya gasps. "Aha?!"

Rose stares at Yaya and through her tears, narrates part of her life story. It is not a pretty scene and several times she stops to sob. Yaya let her spill it all out.

When it is obvious Rose is not saying anymore, Yaya sighs and says, "But you're strong. One can never know you ever went through this kind of life."

Rose sniffs. "You see why Dr. Ashi can never marry someone like me. Even if he wants, his family will never agree."

Yaya rubs her chin. "You just think so. Your determination is enough to attract him to you. If he hears…"

Rose falls on her knees. "Hey, I can't tell him. Please don't tell him. I beg you for God's sake."

Yaya gasps. "Me? I can't tell him. You will tell him yourself."

Rose slides back to her seat. "I can't tell him."

Ashi drives up to the front of the hostel and goes inside. He soon exits with Rose. They get into his car and drive off.

They go to a popular 'point and kill' fresh fish joint, notorious for its mouth-watering smoked fish. Over the sumptuous meal, they laugh and make jokes and have a really good time.

Ashi drops Rose off at the hostel, with gratitude for keeping his company.

Rose enters the room and turns on the lights, and tiptoes to her bed. Yaya is totally covered under her sheet. Rose starts to undress.

Yaya turns sleepily and looks at her. "Did you tell him?"

Rose removes her earrings. "I told you I can't tell him. Goodnight."

Yaya blinks. "Did you catch fun though?"

Rose chuckles. "A lot."

Yaya drags her sheets over her head, and Rose laughs. She sits on her bed and stares into space.

CHAPTER TWELVE

A group of three men, one in his fifties, while the other two are in their twenties, and two women both in their twenties, walk into the village of Imale II. They're dressed in T-shirts and jeans and carry backpacks and look tired.

Villagers come out of their huts and stand by their doorsteps and stare at the group. The group walk through the length of the village and stop under a big tree. They drop their backpacks and follow it down to the ground.

Pastor Gladness, the oldest and leader of the group pass water round and they all drink from the same bottle.

"Brethren, God is your strength," Pastor Gladness says.

Sherry, one of the ladies yawn. "Pastor, I don't know where on earth this is but I just pray these villagers will not eat us alive."

Pastor chuckles. "I understand how you feel."

Temisan, the second lady frowns. "So, what next now?"

Truth, one of the younger men look around. "They'll come to us. You'll soon see one outspoken man will come and ask us what we want."

Temisan gasps. "That sounds scary. Huh, Pastor, I can't believe I just hiked for six hours straight."

Truth chuckles. "My first journey was twelve hours. I can never forget."

Sherry screeches. "Twelve hours! Ah God forbid."

Pastor smiles. "You won't even know. Or did you know this one?"

Temisan and Sherry shriek. "Yes, Pastor!"

They all laugh over the joke.

Truth notices first. "Someone is coming. I said it."

Pastor nods. "Good. He'll take us to the chief."

—

Okong walks up to the group with an arrogant swag and begins to converse in the local dialect. Sly, the youngest in the group and an indigene of one of the neighbouring villages who has long since become a Christian and now works with the missionaries, replies and translates to them.

Sly tells them the chief wants to know who they are and Okong has introduced himself as one of the sons of the most influential men in the village. Pastor Gladness is delighted they can meet the chief. It means they can know if they are welcome to hold a crusade in the village or not.

Okong leads the missionaries to the village Chief, who magnanimously allows them to use the village square to hold their meetings as long as they do not force anyone to attend. It is a prayer answered.

The following morning, the missionaries walk from house to house to invite the villagers to the meeting at the village square. There is a small gathering of people in the open square and pastor preaches to about ten people most of them are children.

After the meeting at the village square, Pastor Gladness, Truth, Sherry and Temisan visit Cholufor's house. As the seeming most affluent man in the village, Pastor Gladness feels it necessary to minister the word of God to him personally.

Pastor raises his voice in front of Cholufor's house. "Una well done o. I dey greet."

A deep male voice answers from within the house. "Na who eh?"

"We be pastor from the church," Pastor says.

Okong comes out tying a wrapper. "Na which church dat?"

"We be from…"

Okong sneers. "Oh, the people. Wetin you dey find? Una don finish your church?"

Pastor nods. "Yes. We wan invite you for the evening service."

Okong stands akimbo. "We no dey come."

Pastor shrugs. "Na just to sidon look. You no go…"

"Pastor, we no dey come." With that said, Okong turns around and walks back into the house.

Sherry sighs. "Wow. This na true ministry o. Choi."

Pastor smiles. "They're not even violent, and the chief allowed us to preach. That is great mercy."

Temisan does the sign of the cross. "God is our strength."

CHAPTER THIRTEEN

A woman from the village holds a heavily pregnant Undeana by the waist and rushes her through the village path. Undeana is in pain and cannot move as fast as the woman helping her.

They approach Cholufor's compound and the woman shouts. "Bring water. Bring cloth…" She disappears into the house with Undeana.

Soon loud labour screams are heard from within. And then a short laughter, and nerve-wrecking wailing.

Later in the evening, Cholufor sits outside on his rocking chair and Uteye comes to serve him food.

Uteye frowns. "This is the second baby she will born dead. Are you sure this girl is not bad luck to this family?"

Cholufor grunts. "And if she is bad luck, what do you want to do about her? Kill her?"

"Ah, why? As long as her bad luck no reach me and my children."

Cholufor glares at her. "Then leave it alone."

Uteye sulks. "The children in the village are afraid of her."

Cholufor growls. "Leave it alone, Uteye."

—

Pastor Gladness and Temisan arrive at Cholufor's compound.

Pastor raises his voice. "Una well done o. Good day. Na mama pikin we dey find. Undeana."

Undeana walks out looking weak and still pregnant. "Good day."

Pastor clasps his hands together. "Sorry. About your baby."

Undeana stares into space, her eyes are empty.

Temisan mumbles, "Sorry."

Pastor exchanges looks with Temisan. "My sister here, Temisan na nurse. She wan check you."

Undeana's eyes flare. "Check me?"

Pastor nods. "Yes."

Temisan tilts her head back. "To be sure you are fine."

Pastor nods again. "She go just ask some questions..."

Undeana swallows. "Cholufor sabi say you dey here?"

Temisan frowns. "Cholufor?"

Pastor presses his lips together. "Her husband." He looks at Temisan. "The old man." He turns to Undeana. "We no tell am say we dey come. As we hear say your pikin die yesterday as you dey born am, and your family no come church, we say make we come see you for ourself."

Undeana raises her chin. "Make you come when Cholufor dey." She turns, pauses as though not sure of her action, and then walks back into the house.

Temisan looks at Pastor. "That went well."

Pastor shrugs. "We'll return when her husband comes back."

Pastor Gladness alone return later in the evening after the service they hold daily. Cholufor offers him a seat outside the house with him.

Pastor tries to convince Cholufor their intentions are pure. "All we want to do is to help her, Cholufor."

Cholufor grunts in a characteristic manner. "Help her how? The gods have not smiled at her. When they do, she will have a child of her own."

"We have a nurse in our team. All she will do is talk to her. Maybe there's something she eats or does that makes her to lose her baby," Pastor says.

Cholufor growls. "I am not an illiterate, pastor. I lived in Calabar and Lagos for many years. I served in the Nigerian army too. I know the work of a nurse. And my woman does not need a nurse."

Pastor sighs. "Can we just chat with her?"

Cholufor lowers his voice. "Do you want me to send Okong after you? It looks like your stay in this village has been too long."

"No, that will not be necessary." Pastor sighs. "She is your money woman, right? You think you will have to spend money on her. If she was your wife, you will let us see her."

Cholufor sits up, his body rigid. "I can do what I like with her. She's my money. It's not about spending money or not."

Pastor refuses to be intimidated. "Then why don't you let us..."

Cholufor leaps to his feet. "Pastor, be on your way."

"We are praying for you. And your family." Pastor rises slowly and stops short when he sees Undeana at the entrance.

He walks into the night feeling a great burden in his heart.

Later that night, Undeana sneaks up to the abandoned shed where the missionary group are fast asleep. She goes to tap Temisan.

Undeana whispers. "Abeg, make una look me now."

Temisan startles. "Pastor!"

Pastor wakes. "Undeana! What are you doing here?"

Temisan sits up. "She wants us to examine her now."

Pastor looks around nervously. "Okay. Temisan, can you ask her the necessary questions as fast as possible?"

"Yes. Yes." Temisan looks at Undeana. "How old are you?"

Pastor shrugs. "She may not know that."

"I know. I am 15."

Temisan bites her lower lip. "How many times you don get belle?"

"Four."

Temisan sucks in her breath. "How many pikin you get?"

"I no get pikin."

CHAPTER FOURTEEN

U ndeana walks stealthily to the door of the house and startles when Okong grabs her hand.

"Where are you coming from?"

Undeana gasps. "I go piss."

Okong snaps. "You go sleep with the pastor and his broda."

Undeana tries to free her hand. "No o. I no go dia."

"You tink say I no see as you waka?"

Undeana shakes her head. "Na piss I go..."

Okong slaps her hard across her face. Undeana screams. The slap is followed by many others.

Several days pass, and Cholufor becomes ill. The village native doctor visits once to give him concoctions and recommend that he gets a lot of fresh air. But when he is seated on his normal rocker outside, he shivers so much from cold, so he is covered in a big wrapper. Uteye, Caro and Undeana take turns in bringing water for him to drink.

Pastor Gladness arrives with the missionaries. Cholufor is covered from head to toe. He shivers badly under the wrapper. Uteye sits beside him.

Pastor fixes his eyes on Cholufor. "I dey greet o."

Uteye rubs a balm from the native doctor on Cholufor's feet. "Una welcome o."

Pastor squats beside her. "We hear say Cholufor dey sick. We say make we come visit."

Uteye steals a wary glance at the group. "Welcome."

Pastor points at Temisan. "Our sister here na nurse. She wan give am medicine."

Uteye frowns at Temisan. "We don dey give hot drink with native leaf."

Pastor looks at Cholufor who is shivering badly, and his eyes are closed. "But dat wan fit no help am."

Uteye pouts. "Na wetin don dey help am since."

Pastor sighs. "You go gree make we pray with am?"

Uteye shrugs. "Anyhow you wan do. Na make him e well be my own."

Pastor looks at his team. "Shall we pray?"

Early the following morning, Uteye runs out of the house wailing.

"Make una hep me o. My own don finish o. Abeg o! Cholufor no dey breath." Uteye throws herself on the ground and rolls. "Hep me o! Make una hep me o!"

Villagers run out of their huts and into Cholufor's house.

By late afternoon, the compound is brimming with villagers. Some are seated on the ground in front of the house, some pace, some roll on the ground, weeping. The richest man in Imale II is dead.

Uteye, Caro, Undeana, and two other women are seated on the ground by one side. Caro carries a baby and two other toddlers sit close around her. Uteye and the other women also have children seated with them. Undeana sits alone. People troop in, greet and leave.

—

Pastor Gladness and the missionaries are in the shed. "We need to really pray. This village has to be won for Christ. It's not enough that the women and children alone are attending our services. We need the men to come too."

Sly sighs. "Pastor, the news going round is not good."

Pastor frowns. "What news?"

Sly shrugs. "I hear murmurs. They say your prayers killed Cholufor. Uteye has been spreading the word and trying to get the people to chase us away."

Pastor exclaims. "Good God."

Temisan smirks. "What's the big deal about that? Of course, the chief can't believe that."

Sly shakes his head. "The chief will believe if they say it long enough."

Pastor frowns. "When did this rumour start?"

"Since two days now. Immediately Cholufor died," Sly says.

Sherry wraps her arms around her body. "What are we going to do?"

Pastor frowns. "We wait."

The following morning, as the team are having morning devotion, Sly rushes in.

"We have to leave. Pastor, the chief has sent the message."

Truth frowns. "Shouldn't we go and see him and explain…"

Sly moves to his backpack and knock a bucket of water over. "No. It's better we leave first. Cholufor was their richest man in this village. Any rumor that he was killed has not gone down well." He pushes his clothes into the bag, ignoring the mess on the ground.

Sherry snickers. "What nonsense rich man?"

Truth frowns. "Don't talk like that."

Temisan looks at Pastor. "Pastor?"

"Begin to pack up."

—

Family members of Cholufor gather in the compound.

An elder addresses the group. "With Cholufor dead, I am now the head of this family. Cholufor has made it clear how he wants his property to be shared before he died." He looks round. "Okong will own his father's farms and all his cows and goats. He will also take the house and allow Suffer to live in the house. Uteye will go back to her father's house with her children. Caro, Mowu, and Ekaitsor will now belong to Suffer with their children." The elder fixes his gaze on Okong. "Okong will own Undeana according to his request to his father."

CHAPTER FIFTEEN

The missionaries walk on the village path, singing a solemn chorus. Undeana jumps out of the bush in front of them.

Pastor steps back, his arms spread to protect his group. "Undeana. What are you doing here?"

Undeana breathes heavily. "I want to come with you."

Pastor sighs. "Ah, what about your family?"

Undeana looks around wildly. "I don't have family. Please don't leave me in this village."

Pastor looks at the others.

Sly steps forward. "Pastor, we cannot take her. She is a money woman. It is a taboo to take a money woman from her husband."

Temisan raises her voice. "But the man is dead!"

Sly shrugs. "Even though."

Temisan comes to stand beside Pastor. "Pastor, we cannot leave her."

Sly looks at Pastor. "We will never be allowed back here if we take her. And if they find her with us. They can kill all of us."

Sherry gasps. "But they will never find her with us. Once we get back to base, we take her out of state."

Truth murmurs, "Who will care for her?"

Undeana squares her shoulder. "I can care for myself." She fixes her eyes on Temisan. "Please."

Sly shakes his head. "Pastor, we can't. I know what I am saying. These are my people and they can be vicious."

Truth groans. "Especially that her family."

Temisan touches Pastor. "Pastor, please. This is the ministry we are here for. It is not only to preach and see them saved but also to help and protect."

Sly comes to stand right in front of Pastor. "We will not be protecting her by taking her. We will be endangering her life. Even if they don't harm us, they will kill her."

Temisan shouts at Sly. "How are you sure about that? How do you know they will find her?"

Sly lowers his gaze. "Once they discover she's missing."

Tears pool in Sherry's eyes. "Pastor please. Let's believe God for protection."

Sly raises his voice. "I believe God too but..."

Pastor speaks softly, his tone negotiating. "Please go back to your village, Undeana. We don't want any trouble."

Sherry and Temisan scream. "Pastor!"

Pastor looks at them. "Please let's get on the way."

They walk past Undeana, who is left on the path shivering, glaring at them.

The missionaries continue in stone silence and after about an hour of hiking, stop under a tree. The ladies sit together, sulking. The men sit together too.

Sly observes the sky. "We still have two hours of sensible light. If we just eat a light meal now, we can make it."

Sherry snaps. "I'm not able to walk again."

Sly looks at her. "Once we rest a little."

Temisan hisses. "I wish I never came on this journey."

Sly shakes his head. "Well, that is sad. This is what ministry is all about."

Temisan flares. "Is ministry about throwing a 15-year old girl who has had four pregnancies and no children back to the people who hate her?"

Sly raises his voice. "Ministry is about applying wisdom. Taking your life as serious as that of others."

Pastor speaks with a soft steely voice. "It's enough, both of you."

Sherry sniffs. "I will never understand."

Pastor looks at all of them one by one. "Let me make you understand, Sister Sherry. And Sister Temisan."

Sly taps Pastor. "Pastor please, can I just tell them a little about our culture?

Pastor nods. "Please do."

Sly shuts his eyes for a moment and when he opens them, they are red and awash with unshed tears. "The money marriage dates back to the beginning of time for our people. It's a culture civilization has not been able to break." He swallows. "A money woman is 'married' to the man who paid for her. Some money women are bought for as little as five thousand naira, and she belongs to her owner for life.

"Even at the man's death, she continues to be his property and will be willed to whomever he desires."

Sherry hisses. "God forbid."

Temisan gasps. "That's slavery."

Sly frowns. "Think of this like a house or car. In these parts of the country, men who buy women show them as a sign of wealth. Undeana's husband had four of them. The only other person in the village who has more than one has only two."

Temisan widens her eyes. "Did I hear you say *only* two?"

"Just for the sake of making reference. I know a man who had nine of them." Sherry and Temisan inhale sharply.

"A money woman's children are the property of her owner. You'll think her welfare is also her husband's duty but it is not. She has to fend for herself," Sly says.

"That's why Undeana probably said she can take care of herself," Pastor says softly.

"She has to find her own food, and for her children, if any, and her husband. She may engage in trading including her body, farming, begging or any other means she finds," Sly says.

Sherry shakes her head. "I'm not sure I can hear any more of this."

Truth shrugs. "If you don't hear, how do we imagine we can help them?"

"A money woman is subject to her owner's whims and wishes and he can do and use her for whatever he desires. He can sell her; sleep with her, pimp her to others and whatever else." Sly's voice sounds like from a distance.

Sherry sobs. "Oh my God."

Sly continues. "And if she escapes, her owner reserves the right to punish her anyway he wishes. It is believed that the 'gods' of the land will kill any money woman who runs away and is not found by her owner."

Temisan cut in. "That is total nonsense."

Sly's lips trembles. "But the people believe it."

Temisan sneers. "How will any gods kills her? What nonsense gods?"

Sly waves his hands in the air. "Look at these hills. How do you imagine a young girl who has never left home will survive in this terrain. If they die of hunger, or never return home, it is assumed the gods have killed her. And listen to this." He swallows. "When a money woman dies, the owner reserves the right to demand his money back from her seller or get a replacement."

Sly clenches his teeth. "And I have seen money women as young as 8 years old. My mother was a money woman."

CHAPTER SIXTEEN

Pastor Gladness stands in front of a large congregation and preaches passionately with power point on a projector. He shows pictures of Undeana, and Cholufor and many other young girls held in the middle of the evil money marriage.

The church is caught up in the midst of all the emotion and many of the members burst into tears. Pastor Gladness speaks passionately and convincingly about the need to eradicate this evil culture.

"We need money, and we need people. We need schools in these areas. We need to empower these people."

Many people come forward to show their support after the service while Pastor Gladness sits with the host pastor, Pastor Elijah, in his office. A well-dressed pretty woman knocks on the open door and walks in.

She curtseys. "Good morning, Pastor. Can I have a moment please?"

Pastor Elijah ushers her in eagerly. "Good morning, madam. Please come in."

"Thank you, sir."

Pastor Elijah waves toward a seat. "Please sit down."

"My name is Eka Pepple. And I know you probably don't know me that well." She chuckles. "I've been hiding a little in church."

Pastor Elijah smiles. "Pleased to meet you, Sister Eka."

"I really enjoyed service today." She looks at Pastor Gladness. "Thank you for that presentation, sir."

"Thank you, madam."

Eka sits forward. "I want to support the missions. My husband and I don't have much, but we can raise help. We want to free all those girls from their money marriage."

Pastor Gladness claps. "Ah! Glory be to God. Glory be to God!"

After Eka leaves the office, Pastor Gladness calls on Sly and shares the good news.

"God indeed is great. The sisters will be very glad." Sly smiles. "This is what I was trying to tell them. If we take that girl, we will never be able to enter that village again. We will just jeopardize our whole mission."

Pastor Gladness nods. "You're right."

"We need to be organized, to plan, strategize. Not just snatch one girl out of the village," Sly says.

"How do we go about it, Bro. Sly? Do we go to their husbands individually?"

Sly moans. "No, Pastor Gladness. Can you take the goods of a strong man without first binding the strong man? Our culture is very stiff on this. We need to tread softly. We go after them one by one."

"How do you mean?"

"It sounds sad, but some of these money women don't want to leave," Sly says.

Pastor widens his eyes. "You can't mean that!"

"I do, pastor," Sly says. "We can start with Undeana who is willing to leave but with her husband dead, we have to find out who she has been willed to."

Pastor's head drops to his chest. "Dear Lord."

Sly jolts. "Thank you, Holy Spirit. An idea just came to me. We can also pass through her family. If we can find who sold her."

Pastor jumps to his feet. "There is work to do, Sly. God has shown us His faithfulness. We need to return to the field first thing tomorrow morning."

Sly throws a salute. "Yes pastor."

CHAPTER SEVENTEEN

Pastor Gladness and Sly enter Kundeve village as dusk sets in and villagers return from their farms. They speak to a passer-by who points toward Undeana's mother's house.

Pastor Gladness and Sly walk up to the house.

Pastor calls out. "I dey salute o!"

Ezor walks out of the house, half naked with his wrapper held tightly in his hand.

"Good day," Ezor says, and looks at them with scrutiny. "Una dey find na who?"

"Undeana's mother."

Ezor frowns. "You dey find am say na wetin happen?"

Sly steps forward and speaks the local dialect. "Who are you?"

Ezor raises his voice. "You na who?"

"We be na church people. We wan see Undeana's mother," Sly says.

Ezor folds his arms. "She no dey. E don go Cameroon with im pikin dem all."

Pastor looks at Sly. "Which day she go return?"

Ezor smirks. "I no no me."

"You be her broda?" Sly says.

Ezor nods. "Yes. You dey find am na for wetin?"

"You sabi who give Undeana do money marriage?" Sly says.

—

Ezor arrives Cholufor's house in Imale II village late in the evening. He's taken the journey urgently and feels weak and tired.

He finds a bench in front of the house and rests a while before raising his voice to greet.

"Una dey well?"

Okong walks out of the house. "Ezor, the fool. Wetin carry you come for this kin time?"

Despite his weariness, Ezor jumps to his feet. "You are mad, Okong. And this time I will deal with you."

Okong's lips twitch. "Get out of my compound."

"Your compound!" Ezor snickers. "Call your father for me."

Okong raises his eyebrows. "I see you have not been travelling for some time or your news carriers would have told you Cholufor died two years ago!"

"Two years!" Ezor lowers himself to the bench. "Cholufor dead?"

Okong chews on his lower lip. "Is he owing you?"

Ezor frowns. "Wetin happen to Undeana, his money woman."

Okong raises his chin. "She's mine now."

Ezor gags and Okong bursts into laughter. "Yes. You can imagine," Okong says.

Ezor braces himself. "Please Okong, be kind, and be a man. For once. Please."

The laughter freezes on Okong's face. "You want my money woman?"

Ezor gesticulates wildly. "No. No. Not at all. Ah. No o. But her mother is sick. She sent me to bring her."

Okong clenches his jaw. "You fool. You want to take her and sell to someone else. You think I am foolish like you."

Ezor stands. "No no. Why will I come all this way to deceive you? If I don't bring her back in four days, kill me."

"You know I will." Okong raises his voice. "Undeana!"

Undeana comes out, carrying a baby in her arms. Her face is puffy, and she looks sick.

"Go prepare yourself. You follow Ezor first thing in the morning," Okong says to her. She nods and walks back into the house. Okong follows her with a lusty gaze.

"Four days, Ezor. Or I will find both of you. And kill you."

CHAPTER EIGHTEEN

Rose follows other students on ward round with other doctors. Ashi walks up to the ward window and stays there, watching Rose and smiling to himself.

Abai walks up behind him. "Lovestruck. The boss needs your attention."

"I can't help myself. The girl is too fine." Ashi pushes away from the window and follows Abai down the corridor. "So what does Daddy want me for?"

Abai chuckles. "Do I know? Didn't you two leave the house together?"

Ashi shrugs. "Now I'm serious about getting married, I have to find my own accommodation."

"No be small tin."

They part ways at the end of the corridor, and Ashi knocks on a door and enters his father's plush office. Dr. Anusa is seated behind his large mahogany desk, his glasses perched on his nose. He's the older version of Ashi, and still looks strong and fit, though he is in his sixties.

Dr. Anusa looks up and Ashi gives a small bow.

"Dr. Ashi, have a seat," Dr. Anusa says in clipped tones.

Ashi sits. "Yes sir."

Dr. Anusa comes around and pulls another visitor's chair and sits in front of Ashi. "I should have told you this at home, but I wanted to discuss it here, so you understand the import of it."

"Yes sir."

Dr. Anusa takes a deep breath. "His Excellency the governor invited me to his office last night. He wants to make me commissioner for health."

Ashi jumps to his feet and bows. "Ah Daddy. Congrats. This is a great stride."

Dr. Anusa smiles. "Yes. Thanks, Ashi. But it means I can't be here often again. You have to take over most of my work. I thank God you are well-qualified, and soon you will be a consultant. You have what it takes to take Hope Hospital higher."

Ashi falls on one knee. "Daddy..."

Dr. Anusa pulls him up. "Stand up."

Tears pool in Ashi's eyes and he swipes it off. "I feel so overwhelmed, sir. That you considered me for this because it's a great responsibility. I mean, you could easily employ a director for this hospital but..."

Dr. Anusa pats Ashi's shoulder. "The appointment will be announced this afternoon, and I will be sworn in tomorrow. So your Mummy and I have agreed to have a small party after the swearing in ceremony."

Ashi nods. "That's good sir."

Dr. Anusa jumps to his feet. "Okay. So, you can go back to your work."

Ashi straightens and hugs his father. "Congrats Daddy. You deserve it."

—

Rose rushes through the corridors and enters the canteen. She looks round and sees Yaya at a table with two other students eating and discussing.

Rose waves at the other two and bends to whisper into Yaya's ear. "Come please, follow me."

Yaya smiles her excuse at the others and follows Rose. "Hope nothing. Good or bad?"

Rose walks out of the canteen and pulls her to the side on the corridor. "I'm in trouble."

"What?"

Rose grips Yaya's hands. "Dr. Ashi. It's Ashi."

"What happened to him?"

Rose looks up and shuts her eyes for a moment. "They've made his Daddy a commissioner. In fact, they just announced it on the radio just now."

Yaya sighs. "I understand how you feel." She squeezes her eyes shut and re-opens them. "You have to tell him everything."

Rose lowered her voice to a whisper. "That's not the main thing, Yaya! Ashi proposed to me this morning after telling me about his Daddy's appointment. In fact, he said he wants to announce our engagement at a small party they want to have tomorrow."

Yaya paces a small space. "What did you say?"

"I was just staring at him. I didn't know what to say."

Yaya gasps. "Aha?"

Rose swallows. "He said we'll go out tonight so we can discuss at length."

Yaya grabs Rose's shoulder and faces her squarely. "Tell him. If it won't work, know now before you get too deep."

Later in the afternoon, Rose and Yaya walk into the room. They go to their beds and drop their bags. Rose sits and twists her hands nervously.

"You're overworking yourself over this issue, Rose. What could be so bad?" Yaya says.

Rose has tears in her eyes. "I can't do this. I should just disappear, so he won't see me again."

Yaya shakes her head. "How do you hope to do that? This guy loves you, it is obvious or he won't ask for marriage."

CHAPTER NINETEEN

I t is late in the evening and Ezor lounges in front of Mam's house, drinking from the best palm wine money can buy. Mam is still not back from Cameroun but Ezor doesn't really mind.

The church people had shocked him when they provided the fifty thousand he requested for Undeana. He knows what he plans to do with it. And what to tell Okong. No man will resist his story. He has planned it all. It's the fourth day now since he took Undeana. Tomorrow morning, Okong will leave Imale II and arrive in the evening. By then, Mam's compound will be full of wailing women. Okong will have no choice but accept the story of Undeana's demise.

Ezor lifts the keg of palm wine to his mouth again. Money indeed is so good.

"Ezor, where is my wife?"

Ezor freezes and lower the keg from his mouth slowly. Only one man on earth has that voice. He staggers to his feet and looks at the deadly eyes of Okong, menacing as ever even in the moon light.

No one needs to advise a man like Ezor in times like this. The wicked Okong. He has thought ahead and known he would not bring Undeana back. Oh, the plans! What would he do now?

He really has nothing to say to Okong. Undeana is gone! The pastor took her out of the village the following day. They didn't tell Ezor where they were taking her. After paying fifty thousand on a girl's head, they can use her for rituals, and no one will question them.

Ezor thinks of only one thing to do. Run. He flings the keg of palm wine at Okong and takes to his heels.

He runs as fast as he can but Okong catches up with him and beats him with his bare hands.

—

Okong picks up the limp body of Ezor and flings him into bush. The moon has gone to sleep, and the village is totally dark. If anyone heard of the assault, they didn't show it because no one came out to rescue Ezor. No one could have anyway.

Okong stands there breathing hard for a long time, and then goes back into the village to search for Undeana. If he doesn't find her here, he will search the neighbouring villages. She will not escape him.

"My father's money cannot just go like that."

—

Pastor Gladness parks his car in front of the church in Calabar and alight with Sly, Undeana and her baby. They are met by Pastor Elijah and Eka. They all walk into the building.

CHAPTER TWENTY

Ashi and Rose stroll through the beautiful serene Marina resort, holding hands.

"Ashi, you know I've been saying over and over again that I'm not in your class."

Ashi sighs. "And I have been saying it over and over that it's in your imagination."

Rose steals a glance at him. "I have my reasons, and after your proposal today, I feel you should know my reasons too."

Ashi shrugs. "It doesn't make any difference to me but since you must say it."

"And the stuff you told me about your job and so on... The day issues come up about me, you won't be happy if you don't know. Because that's how life is."

"I'm hearing you."

"And if after I tell you, you feel we should part ways, feel free and tell me straight. Don't feel bad. I'm ready for the worst."

Ashi shrugs. "Okay."

"I really like you but I have to clear every air between us so we won't have secrets between us in case you decide to continue."

Ashi rolls his eyes. "Say this thing this woman."

Rose takes a shuddering breath. "Okay."

Ashi stops and faces her. "Before you do, I want you also to know there's no perfect person. And from the first day I saw you, my soul wanted you. And I want you to trust me that no matter how shocking is what you want to tell me, I love you. I don't know what your secret is but all my heart is with you. And if I hesitate tonight, or react in shock, know deep down that it's only human nature, and I love you very much. Because just like you said..."

Rose throws back her head. "Ah brother, let's talk the talk before it runs away."

Ashi laughs. "So, you're itching to say it."

Rose draws a deep breath. "I am from Kundeve. One small village more like a bush path. We didn't have up to 30 houses in my village. And my real name is Undeana. But it was changed to Rose when I was brought to school here."

Ashi stares at her, his attention focused solely on her.

"My parents had five of us before my father died in the farm. They believe his cousin killed him out of jealousy."

Ashi nods then shakes his head.

"My mother got pregnant for a man in the village after that, but she didn't marry him. Then she got pregnant again. For another man."

Ashi squints but remains quiet.

"She was still pregnant when I left home at the age of 12..."

—

In a small cocktail party, Rose and Yaya are part of the guests. They stick close together as guests move round. At some point, Dr. Anusa hits his wine glass with a spoon.

"Attention! Attention please." The room quiets down. "We have an important announcement. God is doing great and mighty things for us here today." He summons Ashi at the end of the room. "Ashi, come here."

Ashi goes to take Rose's elbow and lead her forward. "I didn't sleep last night." Some people mumble and laugh. "Not because I was on call. But because of this beautiful, well-mannered lady, Rose Undeana Christopher." There is spattering claps. "My fiancée."

The room erupts with thundering claps and cheers.

Dr. Anusa raises his glass. "Rose and Ashi!"

The guests give a chorus response. "Rose and Ashi."

CHAPTER TWENTY-ONE

Ashi and Rose drive up the main road that leads to Kundeve village with the sun high up, and park by the side. Pastor Gladness is with them. They had left Calabar in the early hours of the day and driven six hours.

They come out of the car.

"This path leads into my village." Rose swallows to control tears. "I haven't seen my mother in fifteen years. I don't even know if she's still alive."

Pastor pats her hand. "She is. Our missions continue to work here and other villages. So, I know."

"I'm sure she won't remember me." Rose turns to Pastor. "Thanks for coming with us at such a short notice."

"The pleasure is mine, Rose," Pastor says.

"I'm not sure I can do this. I should have come to find her at least. Alone."

"It was too dangerous for you to come at any time. After what Okong did to Ezor."

Ashi grips her hand. "Let's do it, baby."

The group arrive at Undeana's childhood hut. It looks pretty much the same with several more cracks in the wall. Ashi grips Rose's hands tighter and smiles at her for reassurance.

Pastor raises his voice. "Una dey for house?"

Mam walks out shielding her eyes. "Who dey dia?"

"Na me. Pastor Gladness."

Mam squints. "I no dey fit see well."

Pastor smiles. "I carry your pikin, Undeana come see you. She don get better life. Her pikin don big well well, dey go school for Calabar."

Mam turns to Rose. "Undeana?"

Undeana bursts into loud tears. Ashi hugs her.

—

The traditional marriage of Rose and Ashi holds in Kundeve village. There is a great display of the culture and food of the Cross-River people. Traditional dancers showcase. There is pomp and fanfare. Ezor's parents stand at the entrance of their house and join other villagers to watch. Mam is dressed beautifully, and the house has been repaired. Rose looks extremely beautiful, and Ashi looks handsome. Yaya and other medical students wear a colourful uniform outfit. It is a glorious occasion.

After the traditional marriage, the couple return to Calabar for a church wedding attended by the most important people in Cross River state and Nigeria. Rose and Ashi then proceed on their honeymoon at the Obudu Ranch resort in Cross River state.

—

It's her first day at the Hope Hospital after her wedding and honeymoon and Rose feels light-headed and excited. Her life is finally just the way she wants it. She walks along the corridor of the hospital, humming a hymn softly. People greet her left and right. She smiles at each of them and wave at others. Her school is back in session and she doesn't need to work at Hope anymore, except that now she has chosen to visit as much as her academic work will avail her. Because this is her husband's hospital, for mercy's sake.

Rose gets to a small office, knocks and enters. Ashi is seated behind a desk.

He beams. "Mrs. Rose Anusa. How are you?"

Rose hugs him with a peck. "That's me o. Ah, first day at work after almost four months. I've missed so much."

"As my wife, you have up to a year for your maternity leave. But you'll catch up, I trust you."

"Amen o." She heads for the door. "I just said I should check on my hubby."

Ashi escorts her. "How sweet." He gives her a peck on her neck. "We'll see later?"

"I have a special treat for you when you get home."

Ashi groans. "Ha, I love your special treats. I must close early." He looks up. "God please reduce patients today."

They both laugh at the joke. Ashi opens the door for her she stares at him fondly, backing the corridor, and bumps into someone. The man curses loudly.

Rose turns to apologize and exclaims. "Ezor!" Her eyes pop out in horror. "They said you were dead."

Ezor wears a coverall and carries a bucket and mop. He steps back but it is obvious he has a bad limp. "Undeana!"

Ashi looks from one to the other. "Who is this, calling you by name?"

Rose turns to Ashi with dull eyes. "Ezor. Kundeve Ezor."

Ashi gasps. "He's one of the newly employed janitors!"

A NOTE FROM SINMISOLA OGÚNYÍNKA

This story is fiction based on true events. This is the fairy tale I want for every one of these girls who have been violated by our culture. It is a culture that has defied civilization but where there is light, darkness must not continue to comprehend it.

Please support our campaign and help put a smile on the faces of these innocent children. Each of them can have the fairy tale Rose has.

Rose, is a real child who was bought back for fifty thousand naira as depicted in the fictionalized character. But Rose's fairy tale is still in the making. Many more girls are in the bondage.

The real Rose is in the care of brethren who are devoted to the rehabilitation of these girls, and their family members who have been rescued from this culture.

The second part of this book is about real money women, their raw stories told in their voices.

PART 2
STRANGER THAN FICTION

True tales of girls sold into money marriage.

WARNING!

These are true stories. To retain the gravity of the violation against these girls, the editing in this part of the book is minimal and reduced at most times, to grammatical and punctuation errors. Parts of the stories are as-told by the violated girls. Many of the names are real, especially that of the missionaries working in these communities. This is intentional.

If you are overly emotional, you may be reduced to tears, puking or fainting by the things you are about to read in the next few pages, please be warned.

Though no pun is intended, we have no apology for relating these tales as is.

CHAPTER TWENTY-TWO
BETRAYAL OF TRUST

My name is Dorathy. I am from Ugbakoko II. I was a small girl growing up happily in the village until the day they announced to me that I was going to be taken to my husband's house.

Apart from the fact that I was very young, the age of the man I was going to be married to was more than ten times my age. I refused that I was not going to agree to that kind of marriage.

In spite of the beatings and pressure from my family and distant relations, I told them I would rather die than marry the old man.

A woman came visiting and asked to speak with me. She promised she would take me away where the man would never see me again. I felt I was free.

She took me to a community in Boki. By the following evening, the old man arrived the house. Once he arrived, I ran into the bush through the back door. I slept inside the bush for the night and ate palm fruits during the day for food. They found me and took me back to the house. I hated that woman for lying to me.

By that evening, the woman called me and was saying she was sorry for what had happened. She claimed she had no idea the man was coming that way. I was in the room with her when three other women entered the room. They didn't say a word; even the woman talking too became quiet. Their eyes were fixed on me. Could it be they want to punish me for running away? They are my tribal women, but their quietness was so suspicious and hurting. I began to sense something was seriously wrong. I stood up. "Thank you, mama." As I took a step, someone stepped into the room, blocking the light that filtered in through the door. I adjusted my eyes, wondering what was happening.

It was Philip (real name), the old man!

As if a whistle was blown, the women rushed at me, raised and laid me on the mat, removed my clothes as they held me down. My hands, legs and head were held down as the old man came and had sex with me. The pain was so excruciating.

This act of rape continued before the man went back to the village.

A few weeks later, I began to have strange feeling - vomiting and nausea.

The woman (the man's relation) asked how I was feeling. By the time I told her, she jubilated and announced to me that I was pregnant.

That was how I was 'humbled' and today, I have five children for him. The children are not properly spaced. Some of them are suffering from malnutrition. This man is old and can hardly do any work.

As a money wife, you can't run forever; the man can harm you through the 'rope' (tied during the day the girl is officially handed over. The rope serves as an effigy - as the girl's name is mentioned seven times, the knot is tied. Whatever happens to the rope, translates to the girl wherever she is).

As a money woman, where will you run to - your family? They have sold you already!

Even if the man kills you physically or otherwise...nobody will ask him. You are his money.

We are often told that we are like fowl bought from market and can be slaughtered any time as the need arises.

I am responsible for providing for both my children and my husband.

It is not an easy life.

CHAPTER TWENTY-THREE

INTERVIEW WITH PHILIP BY PASTOR RICHARDS

Pa Philip. (He is the husband of Dorathy II – the girl that was held down by four women…)

Richards: Papa Philip o, you, you go happy say somebody dey sleep ya woman – ya money woman? (*Papa Philip, will you be happy if you hear someone slept with your money woman?*)

Philip: Yes. I wan say if anybody sleep my woman or ada (either any of ma woman at all, if e givi something, make e (the woman) carry the thing come make we chop together. If e come house, make e not be heavy (be heady, stubborn) with me…make e come gentry: e bi say, na ma husband dis, me and im no no het quarrel. (*Yes. If anyone slept with my woman, any of them at all, as long as the woman brings something home to me, and is not stubborn but informs me gently, I won't be offended.)*

Richards: Even if you catch am dey sleep your wife; after e giv your wife something and she bring am. No trouble? *(What if you catch the man with your wife? If she brings something home to you, will you be offended?)*

Philip: If I catch am wey e dey for ma house wey we de sleep one bed, ah! That one na trouble. I no go gree. *(If I catch them on my bed, there will be trouble.)*

Richards: But (I cut in) if na for parlour wey no be for your bed – dat one...no problem? *(But what if you caught them in your parlour, will there be a problem with that?)*

Philip: No problem.

Richards: So why problem go dey if na for your bed? *(So why will there be problem if you catch them in your bed?)*

Philip: Because na dia we dey sleep together. *(Because that's where we sleep together.)*

Richards: So even if e go outside come get belle. You go happy? *(So what if she gets pregnant from another man?)*

Philip: If e go carry belle come for house, if e born, dem go call dat man wey sleep with am? I think dem go call say Philip im woman get belle. How I no go happy? *(If she gets pregnant for another man, do you think they will call that other man's name? I think they'll say Philip's woman is pregnant. How won't I be happy?)*

Richards: You go be happy? *(You'll be happy?)*

Philip: Yes! I go be happy. You think say dat man wey e don be old...all dat im child im woman de born am: dem dey call people name? No be n aim born am o but dem dey call im name. Na me I go giv name say na di pikin name naim be dis. *(Yes! I'll be happy. You think all these old men you see with children are the biological fathers? But everyone calls them by the men's names. If my woman comes to me with pregnancy from another man, I will give that child a name.)*

Richards: Even as you, you sabi say no bi you born the pikin? You go give am... (He cuts in sharply.) *(Even though you know you are not the biological father of the child. You'll give a...) He cuts in sharply.*

Philip: I go giv am name bicos na my wife; e dey for my house. Yes. If you have child, im go hunting for bush, e go kill meat for bush... I think e go come give na you papa? E go carry give another person? Na so for woman: e be say e don go hunting, e don kill meat come giv me. I will take am with two-two hand. I think you see? How I no go be happy say my wife bring something? E dey bring meat, cook am for me I chop. Na my gain. The man wey sleep am e don carry everything? *(I will give the child a name because the woman is my wife. She's in my house. Yes. If your child goes hunting and comes back with meat from the bush, won't he give the meat to his father? Will he give to another person? It's the same with a woman. Going to meet other men outside is like going hunting. Getting pregnant is like coming back with meat from hunting, which she gives me. I will take it with my two hands. Don't you see? How won't I be happy that my wife brought something? She brings meat, cooks it for me, and I eat. It's my gain. The man who impregnated her, has he gained anything?)*

CHAPTER TWENTY-FOUR

GAMBLED INTO MARRIAGE

My name is Gift.

This is what I was told by the man who owns me now; my father is indebted to him.

My father was a gambler.

While others looked for work to do to feed their family, he considered gambling an easy way to make money. This kind of money-making venture was not dependent on strength or too much exertion of energy; but it was always tangible, usable cash when one wins.

He leaves home early and returns late from his 'work'.

One day, I was told, the game did not favor him. When it was his turn to play, he was to play against someone who he usually treats and calls 'wife' during play. This is because the man is not considered an expert; he was always defeated by almost everyone.

But this day was different. This timid, always-defeated fellow beat my father three times in a row – winning four thousand, five hundred naira.

My father borrowed more money. The two more times he borrowed, the two more times he suffered defeat. Nobody agreed to lend him any money again.

The man was ready to end the game, but my father was far from surrendering. All attempts to convince him to leave and fight again another day failed. It was at this point that I was sent for.

I arrived thinking he wanted to send me on errand to my mother in the market as he often did; he rather asked me to stand by the man sitting opposite him.

"This will be the final and deciding game," he said. "I am placing her as bet for five *tasan nara*."

"For who? Your pikin?" the other man asked.

Other men raised objection, but my father said, "This girl na my pikin. Na me bring am for bet for five *tasan nara*. Na wetin I like I go do with my pikin." He pushed me to the man.

The man looked at me from head to toe and said he would play with him for three thousand. The argument went back and forth until they arrived at three thousand, five hundred naira.

"If you win me, you marry am. I go get the money pay you and carry my pikin. No worry. Play!" My father said.

In less than five minutes, the game was decided: my father lost to the man!

"I no tell you? Today na my day. You don see ba? Next time, come flex muscle with me again." The man turned to me. "Small girl, make we go. Until your papa bring my money, you go remain with me." He held my hands and pulled me across the road.

I tried to cry. I was about 7 years old. "Leave me," was all I could mutter. My mind must have gone blank...

I was told that three years later, my father came up with the N3,500 but the man told him the money had appreciated in value with the passage of time coupled with my being fed and cared for, in his house.

I am now grown and still in that compound. I have become one of his wives.

My father is dead and the thought of ever being free is like making a cassava farm in a dessert.

My father's relations have been coming time after time to ask their in-law for one favor or another.

I wish I had a choice in deciding who to marry.

It was a painful season growing up in that compound; the clothes I wore the day I was taken was what I wore for months; my under wear was worn out and torn till I hadn't any to wear.

Nobody even followed to come ask after me.

CHAPTER TWENTY-FIVE

MERCY

I am Mercy. I am from Ugbakoko I. I am a money woman. I do not know when I was given out because I was very small.

This is the story I am told now that I am 13years old.

Mercy's mother was sick, and money was needed to provide medical care (meanwhile, no diagnosis was made as no one took her to any government hospital – no health facility exists in the community but there was one in the local government HQ.

The woman's relative began to worry that she would die if nothing was done. The proper thing was for them to rally round, task themselves and make contributions toward helping their sister... that was not the angle of discussion or thought.

"I think dis wa sista born pikin for you?" the elderly man

in Mercy's mother family asked Mercy's father, Sylvester (real name).

"E born me two woman-pikin. The one don big so ..." using his hands to indicate the height of the first girl child. "The second one still be small."

"E still de suck breast?" He questioned.

"No, e don pass one year and some month wey e no suck breast again. De picken don pass now three years so," Sylvester said.

"E fine so! We no get for waste time. Come here for next two market day; for evening. I go look me for some man wey e buy this pikin. No worry, things go fine." He said as he pulled out his snuff box.

Before the 10th day (market days are counted in 5 days as against the 4 days Igbo market days' system) the elderly man visited and told Sylvester about the arrangement that has been made regarding Mercy. The buyer was ready and waiting.

The following morning, Sylvester set out with Ayam now known as Mercy (3 ½ years old) strapped on his back. He trekked for over four hours across mountains to arrive Yindeve (real name) village.

He was well received and offered a place to rest while they prepared meal for him.

One by one, two by two, they were coming to greet Sylvester and examining their new bride.

In the evening, Sylvester officially explained to Ayam his mission. Over a few bottles of beer and palmwine, they joke and rejoiced on the new relationship welling up between the two families.

All the while, Ayam couldn't leave her father. Not even for one minute. Every attempt to separate them result in her holding on to his hands or trousers, with shouts following.

"Leave am so," an old woman pointed. "Im no shabi say n aim new compound dis."

Tired and weary of the day's activity – strapped on the back to this strange place, following Papa every minute, scared of these strange faces, fighting sleep throughout all afternoon - Ayam finally slept. It was a deep sleep.

"Dis ya pikin, e be like say e get na trong (strong) head o. See how some small pikin come kip we say we no go go fa sleep?" The new mother in-law said as she beckoned on Sylvester to lead him to the room he'd spend the night. Everyone retired to bed; each person bidding Sylvester farewell as they might not see again before his departure for Ugbakoko.

At about 3:30am the following day, Sylvester woke up and woke his "in-law".

"Na go I wan go me now," he said as they exchanged greetings.

"E fine so! Greet me ya pipru (people) all."

"Dem go hear. Make I go quick quick before di man pikin go wake up," Sylvester said as he touched his pocket to make sure the ten thousand naira he was given the night before, was still intact. Secured.

He took the bush path and walked on with the flashlight he had hidden in his inner jacket.

Imagine the trauma the girl Ayam, goes through as she wakes up the following morning to strange unfriendly faces...

Years later, we planted a church in Ugbakoko village. The parents of Ayam gave their hearts to Christ.

As part of our work, we teach the Word of God and teach on family values....how to care for children as they are gifts from God, they are the ones to raise us up when we are old and need help... advocating against girl marriage...the dangers...the slavery nature...the suffering involved...it's a move against God's Word etc...

Sylvester touched by the teachings, went to see the pastor after the Morning Prayer session.

"Pastor Eno (real name), dis thing wey you una de preach am so, e de enter me fine. I bin don de think am say I go tell you something. All dis ma pikin wey de here; e get someone wey e no dey o! We sell am for money marry."

"Sylvester!" Eno was surprised. "Dis one no be talk wey we go stand talk. Come make we sidon for house talk."

After the discussion Pastor Eno assured him she will relay the issue to Pastor Richards...

Apart from praying, we knew it was a dangerous thing to get into especially as we were non-natives.

On my (Richards) way to Esa Cameroon, I decided to pass through Yindeve village. Our missionary in Esa field said he knows the compound well.

On arriving the compound, we entered the house, greeted the mother-in-law and asked for water.

The woman called Ayam to bring us drinking water. I almost shouted as I saw her; the striking resemblance with her father. My camera was put to work before you say, "jack".

The husband also came in to welcome us. In their joys of seeing visitors, I asked if I could snap him...he obliged me.

We stepped into the case, made ten thousand naira available after series of discussion...attempting to allay their fears that nothing will happen to the girl.

They sent for Mercy's uncle (the old man that made the selling arrangement). We had a meeting that lasted for about twenty minutes. We tried to make him see the evil of denying the girl education and exposing her to slavery at such a tender age. After a long pause, he took the money and assured us he will try his best.

He sent back the money a week later.

Mercy's father kept asking our help. Each time we had our students come for scholarship retreats, he would cry, remembering Mercy and the fact that she would have been one of the students. One of those days, he told me how the daughter has become "for general." He explained that people from the compound would come and ask permission from Ayam's husband – some give money - for him to allow her help them carry their fermented cassava or farm produce to the market four or five hours away. Many times, the people would promise her money or some other reward but after they get to the market, they'll abandon her or even threaten to beat her when she complains.

HOW WE GOT HER

Ayam went to the market one day and ran into someone she learnt was from Ugbakoko – her village. She told the woman she was Sylvester's daughter and would like to go greet her father. The unsuspecting woman gave her direction, put her on a bike to take her to the Ugbakoko chief's compound; locating the father's house would not be difficult from there.

Once Sylvester got word that his daughter was home, he ran to Pastor Eno – missionary in Ugbakoko. Eno called Richards who was attending a meeting in Uyo. He called another friend in Obudu and asked him to accommodate the girl until he returns from his trip. Arrangement was made for her to be moved.

Within the two weeks she was away to Obudu, the husband and some family members came looking for her. They wanted their wife back.

We returned her when we couldn't get the family in Obudu to keep her any longer.

We returned her to Ugbakoko but told the parents we would arrest them if the child was released to anybody.

Ayam has been enrolled in the primary school in Ugbakoko - she is in Primary 1 at age 13!

CHAPTER TWENTY-SIX

SNATCHED FROM SCHOOL

I am Vivian. I am a Becheve girl from Mangblan in Kwande Local Government Area of Benue State. I was privileged as a girl to be among the ones chosen to be sent to school by Faith House Missions. My father has always said it was total waste training a girl in school.

When I was in Primary 3, some men visited our compound. One of them registered serious disapproval regarding my being put in school. Since I didn't know what was happening or why he had such boldness to speak, I only assured myself that nothing was big enough to deny me the privilege of education. I continued with going to school.

One morning, an elderly man came in company of two men. My father welcomed and entertained them. In the course of their discussion, my father called me and asked me to stand in front of them.

"Vivian," he started, "you know I am your father and I know what is good for you. Though I have not told you this before, you are now ripe for what man can do with woman. Na your husband this," pointing to the eldest of the visitors.

"*Jesus!*" I shouted. I felt the ground should just open for me to enter... "Papa! How? When? Where have I gone wrong?" I asked with tears rolling down my cheeks. I could not well up enough questions in my confused state.

"My pikin, you no do no nothing. Na so wa people dey do am. Na im I don chop this man im money say make I give am my pikin. E be na good man!" He added.

At this point I made for the opening I saw but one of the young men suspecting my moves quickly held me by wrapper and dragged me to a standstill. All my struggles to break loose only attracted beatings in the name that I was being stubborn to my father.

"Is that what you are taught in that your church?" they bellowed at me.

That was how I was dragged out of my compound and beaten along the road any time I protested.

In the man's compound, life was not too different from what obtained in my community. Poverty and misery seemed to be a next door neighbor. I was kept under watchful eyes. I refused to enter the same room with the man. He made several attempts to talk with me but I would not just listen. I pretended as if I was settling in with the family – he already had two wives each old enough to be my grand-mother.

One of those days, I pretended to be ill and did not follow them to the farm. When they all left, I ran into the bush and tried to straighten out my calculations on the way I was brought in to the community. A few minutes was enough, I did not look back. It took me over four hours of running, making hurried attempts to rest and scooping water from the streams on the way, before I arrived our compound in Mangblan.

On seeing me, my father let out a shout, "Ah heeeee (ahh hay)! You are here. Is there any problem? Did your

husband send you? Why have you come?" He queried.

I cannot explain all the kind of abusive words my father used on me that day as I told him of the hardships I had faced for the period I was in that man's house. He wouldn't want to hear any of that.

A few days after I arrived my village, Pastor Richards came. He heard the story and visited my father. He discussed with my father to let me be, especially since I was being forced into the marriage. After Pastor left unknown to me, my father had sent out word to the man telling him that, "if he didn't come to take me away, he (my father) would not be held responsible for whatever happens regarding the marriage."

I was taking my bath in the village stream when I saw five young men coming down the hill and heading my direction.

"Don't these men have respect for a woman's privacy?" I reasoned.

Before I could raise my voice as I tried to reach for a wrapper to cover my nakedness, they were already at arm's reach: landing slaps on my face and kicking me from every direction. I shouted and wailed. With my house close to the stream, I had thought someone would rush down to see what was happening to me. I did not know these men or where they came from. What have I done? Could this be the Boko Haram people we hear in stories? I shouted the more. By this time, my head was being pushed into the water. I feared for death.

"Man don buy na you, your papa chop im money all, and you e no wan go?" One of them blurted out.

"Oh! It's still this money wife thing. God help me!" I said quietly as I tried to gain my posture, not minding how hard I was hit. One of the men gave me a blow on the back and asked where I was going. I stood speechless.

One of them threw the wrapper at me and said, "Tie dat tin make we go; we dey go na Oga im house na na na."

My heart skipped.

As they pulled me along, I saw to my shock that my father had been sitting down under a shade and listening to all that was happening.

"Pikin wey e no dey hear something. Na so!"

At this time, I knew I was in a lone world. Would my mother have come to my aid if she were to be alive?

I was been led like a goat to the market. I was put in front while the men followed me with whips. Only God can repay those men for the pains they inflicted on me.

I ran again. I feared to go home. I made it out to Amana and headed for Orimekpang. I met some people from my village who go to do clearing jobs for pay.

A young man took interest in me and took me in. To him, he had found a wife of his dream. He really cared for me. He began making arrangement to visit my father when he discovered I was a virgin. To cut the story short, I became pregnant for him.

He got me registered in the PHC (Primary Health Center). The mother was so happy and would ask to know how I faired every day.

My man returned home one day and called me coldly. All attempts to make him eat first, failed. He asked me to tell him the truth about me and my husband. I told him everything.

"So," he said, "this child belongs to that your old husband in that remote village? My love for you, my sweat, my care for you...all for that man? You will have to leave." He told me how some of my tribal people whispered my being a 'money wife' to his hearing.

I returned home. I was shocked to see my father happy for my pregnancy. "No bi dat man im money e don dey bring some profit so? I thank God," he said.

I can't explain all the hardship I faced having and raising this child but I trust God and still believe that one day, things will change for me.

CHAPTER TWENTY-SEVEN

BOUGHT WIDOWED WILLED

My name is Dorathy Etagwa. I am from Katele. As a little girl growing up in the village, I used to hear and see people referred to as "Ukwasi Ngoro." I thought that they, also called "Olambe" (purchased item) was a very good pet name for the "Ukwasi Ngoro' (money wives), cut out for the best of marital lives as they were regarded as the pride of their husbands.

As I wondered about the 'glamour' such position held within a family where one or more wives would have been before the moving in of the husband's pride, I began also to wonder why I was been referred to as 'Ukwasi Ngoro.' Could this be a pet name because of the fondness my father had for me?

In all the times I enjoyed such pet name, I also wondered why I was not allowed to join other children at the village school. I was simply told I was special and would be corrupted by education that will 'open my eyes'. But I loved to see them chant their 'ABCD' and I wanted to know that song too. Each attempt to sneak to school was met with sharp rebukes and heavy beatings.

The euphoria of being labelled 'special' began to vanish when my father called me into his room and told me I was going to be taken to my husband's house.

"Marriage?" I asked.

"Yes, my daughter. Someone has already paid for you. He is my brother and I know he will take proper care of you."

The talk did not make sense to me until he mentioned the name of the man whose wife I had already become since my father had collected both money and other items from him.

"Father, but you have always said this man was your brother?" I asked.

"Yes, my daughter, that is why it is good for you; he is my brother."

I tried to fight the thought of being given out in marriage at an early age to a man older than my father. I cried and cried, tried to appeal to my father. He painted a fearful picture of what will befall me if I refused to go to my husband:

- I will be stripped naked in broad day light; my hands will be tied to my legs, my legs will be tied to a wood used to separate my two legs; seeds of corn from a native doctor will be inserted in to my private part and possessed fowls will come pick up the seeds of corn from the ground and finally from between my legs. The result? Shame and inability to ever bear a child as a woman.

- I have already been sold and do not belong to the family any-more. I had no business enjoying rights that do not belong to me.

- I will be destined to a cruel and slow death

as the gods will ensure I pay dearly for my stubbornness.

- My husband has bought me for a purpose; frustrating it will attract all forms of evil against the family - death for me and my father.

He asked me if I wanted him dead. I was so scared.

My fear gave way to confusion and 'insanity' when he told me that, this man, my husband, was my grand-uncle (my grand-mother's younger brother!)

Was this not an abomination?

Nobody gave any ear to my plea and questions or even my age.

I was forcefully taken to Mangblan where 'my husband' had mi-grated to.

IN MY HUSBAND'S HOUSE

At first, he tried to be very nice to me. Broke palm kernels for me to eat, bought groundnuts, gave me plenty of meat; he even gave me some economic fruits (ogbonor) from his harvest to sell in the market...out of the sales, he gave me permission to buy what I liked. All the kind gestures were gravely attacked by his brothers who felt he had already spent money buying me; why should he be wasting money again on me. This was when my woes multiplied.

I couldn't run away. To whom would I go? I am sold and belong to another man.

When I had my first pregnancy, I had all sorts of pain and fearful experiences. Hospital was not an answer. My husband would hand out twenty or at most fifty naira to me. Whatever drug he gave me, I would take; I couldn't tell what drug they were...they were not in packs, no labels...whether they were expired or not, no one knew.

I lost the pregnancy. Most nights, I felt physical hands pressing my stomach. My husband didn't react when I complained. Any man is free to do whatever he liked with his money wife.

My husband died four years ago. I had always feared that he would die soon; he was old and would always complain of one ache, feeling or another in his body.

Once he died, emptiness and all kinds all frustrations set in. I was never allowed to touch my late husband's economic fruits. My attempt to make oil from ripe palm fruits to care for my sick child got me a beating such as I have never had from my late husband's brother. No one, not even one family member from my house showed concern or came to my rescue.

I was not even allowed to sell cassava from my own farm to take care of myself and my son – a farm I made.

Words are not enough to express the troubles I have gone through in this little life.

After the burial, I was transferred to one of my husband's sons - I am a lot older than him. He has declined taking me as wife.

I am not accepted any more in family. My new husband has done well to reject me. I have no help coming from both ends.

God has helped me through the Church. My welfare has become their responsibility. I now stay in the church facility in another village waiting for the plan to send me out to acquire a skill to materialize.

Knowing Jesus Christ is one of the best things that has happened to me. I now have joy. My head is daily clearing up. I trust God to help me understand His plan for my life in the midst of all that happened to me.

Every year 14 million girls, some as young as 10, are forced into marriage worldwide. And the shocking truth is it's happening right under our noses.

THERE ARE MANY MORE. CAN YOU HELP? WE ARE TRYING BUT WE NEED YOU TO HELP US HELP THEM – *FAITH HOUSE MISSIONS.*

ABOUT THE BOOK AND AUTHORS

THE BOOK

Rose is lied to by her mother that she was being sent to an uncle in another village so she can go to school. Unknown to her, her mother has collected money from a devious cousin who has traded her into marriage. Rose arrives the uncle's place to discover she is now in a money marriage.

The story of Rose is true. But the Money Woman movie has been modified into fiction for a viewing audience. This does not however reduce the effect of this form of menace.

The book, Money Woman, not only consists of the fictional version of Rose's story but true tales from interviews conducted with:

1. Dorathy from Ugbakoko II, sold to a man ten times older than her.

2.

Gift who was gambled for N3,500 (approx. $15) by her father.

3. Mercy from Ugbakoko I who was sold to offset her mother's medical bills before she was 4 years old.

4. Vivian a Becheve girl snatched from school and beaten for resisting marriage.

5. Dorathy from Katele who was bought, widowed and willed.

THE AUTHORS

Sinmisola 'Sinmi' Ogúnyinka is an author, wife, mother, movie producer, and talk-show host. She is also a Craftsman of the Jerry B. Jenkins Christian Writers' Guild, Colorado, USA, and founder of Pleasant Writers' Guild. Sinmi, a graduate of Economics from Obafemi Awolowo University, Ile-Ife, blogs, teaches writing, and has self-published many books with titles such as Frail Flesh, Pepper, and Sister Minister. She lives with her family wherever the Lord leads her husband to plant a church.

Portfolio:

Facebook/Instagram: Sinmisola Ogunyinka

Akonam Chybuikem Richards holds degrees in Missions, Theology and Guidance and Counseling. He served as President, Christian Union (2005/2006) and President, JointCampus Christian Fellowship (2006-2007) in University of Calabar. He has led Faith House Missions in Pioneer Missions since 1992. He is married to Grace and they are blessed with three biological children - Glorypraise, Preach and Chinonso.

Email: _akonams@gmail.com_
Facebook: Richards Chybuikem Akonam

THANK YOU FOR BEING A PART OF OUR JOURNEY.

THE CAMPAIGN AGAINST THE MONEY WOMAN COMMENCED IN 2015.

PLEASE READ:

EVERY CENT FROM THE SALE OF THE BOOK "MONEY WOMAN" WILL GO INTO THE CAMPAIGN AGAINST THE MONEY WOMAN SCOURGE. WE COVET YOUR SUPPORT. PLEASE BUY AND SUPPORT.

www.ingramcontent.com/pod-product-compliance
Lightning Source LLC
Chambersburg PA
CBHW031006210726
48290CB00007B/2500